Dad isn't looking at me, but he isn't moving.

"Don't, Jim." Byron's shaking his head. "Don't say bad things."

But I'm chock-full of bad things, eight years' worth. "You! I'm talking to you!" Dad knows who I'm talking to. I'm leveling at him over Byron's head. "You leave him alone. You gave up your rights to him. You walked out before you ever heard his voice. You think you can make that up now with a couple of stinking aspirin?"

FATHER FIGURE

RICHARD PECK

LAUREL-LEAF BOOKS bring together under a single imprint out-standing works of fiction and nonfiction particularly suitable for young adult readers, both in and out of the classroom. Charles F. Reasoner, Professor Emeritus of Children's Literature and Reading, New York University, is consultant to this series.

Published by
Dell Publishing
a division of
The Bantam Doubleday Dell Publishing Group, Inc.
666 Fifth Avenue
New York, New York 10103

The trademark Laurel-Leaf Library® is registered in the U.S. Patent and Trademark Office.
ISBN: 0-440-20069-5

RL: 5.9

Reprinted by arrangement with Viking Penguin, Inc.

Printed in the United States of America

March 1988

10 9 8 7 6 5 4 3 2

KRI

This book is for
Robert Unsworth
George Nicholson
Richard Brundage
and for
Madeline and Sam Paetro

One

When my mom died, I spent a lot of time—maybe too much—trying to visualize how it happened. My kid brother, Byron, was going over it in his mind too, in his own way. Even at a distance I like to believe I can hear him thinking, and I thought I ought to be ready if he ever asked me anything.

When somebody dies alone, you try to fill in the details, maybe to make up for not being there and changing the whole history of the thing. It's one of those times you want to be able to account for. An alibi for some higher authority than the police: *James Atwater, where were you on the night of April twenty-ninth between the hours of . . .*

It was a Tuesday night, symphony night for my grandmother. She'd gone to the Brooklyn Academy of Music with her friend, Mrs. Schermerhorn. They've got season tickets, and they've sat in the same two seats every week for maybe thirty-five, forty years. Mrs. Schermerhorn lives on Joralemon Street, directly behind us. Her old stretched Cadillac Fleetwood is garaged in the alley between. Her garage doors face ours.

I can picture Nathan, her chauffeur, nosing the old Fleetwood out of the alley that Tuesday evening, braking at the corner, the red taillights turning the alley red. Swinging around to Joralemon Street to pick up Mrs. Schermerhorn on her front steps. Then doubling back and creeping up Remsen Street, where my grandmother always waits in the bay window, leaning on her Lucite cane and looking at her watch.

That night my brother, Byron, had gone with a bunch of kids from his school and somebody's father to the Botanic Garden to see a display of bonsai trees, those little stunted trees the Japanese train down to potted plants, miniature versions of the real thing. Byron's not particularly into stunted trees, but anything interests him. At the age of eight he's picked up weird snatches of higher learning from somewhere. Where, I couldn't say. That isn't the way my mind works.

I was all the way up in the Bronx in Van Cortlandt Park that night. It's down the hill from my school, the Van Cortlandt Academy for Boys. Our playing fields are across Broadway at the edge of the park. There's a hill farther in, where one of Washington's generals lighted signal fires during the Revolutionary War. The place is full of cross-country runners, West Indians playing cricket on their own pitches, and our ball diamonds.

I'm kind of sub-coach for the Lower School ball team. Not what you'd call a team. Put it this way: I'm father figure for our own Bad News Bears. We practiced late that night because the floods were on in the park in spite of the energy crisis. The little guys thought being out this late was a big deal. I never pushed athletics with Byron, who doesn't even go to my school. What he wants he takes on his own, and you can push a kid only so hard.

I had a couple fourth graders off to one side swinging leaded bats for muscle building, and a double row of fifth graders organized to play pepper. Then I gave my sixth graders a little running commentary on the rock-bottom basics, like don't bunt into short grass, and try to hit to the right if there's a man on second. We don't get much past the fundamentals. Not with a self-taught coach who learned to slide by watching the ground come up at him. I don't know if they learn anything, but they like the attention.

When it got really dark, some of the younger ones started glancing up at the sky and out past the lights. So I yelled for them to wrap it up and get all the equipment together. I wear this chrome whistle on a lanyard the kids gave me for a present, but I never use it. I'm not that much of a coach type. So I just yell a lot. But they like to see me wearing the whistle as a badge. They grouped up in a convoy behind the two biggest sixth graders for a walk to the subway. They're committed to their tough image, but none of them wants to tackle the subway alone at that age. I wouldn't want them to, anyway.

I stayed on in the park by myself, running the bases a few times, practicing my hook slide which is reasonably dependable but nothing to look at. Then it got too dark even for me. You could see the white legs of people pumping along the park paths in the distance, but in New York you don't know if they're jogging for health or running for help. I took the subway home, grabbed something to eat out of the refrigerator since Almah wasn't on duty in the kitchen, and went up to bed. Probably I figured my mom was already asleep. She needed a lot of rest by then.

So once I account for everybody else, I have to think about how Mom died. That's what's left. She died in her car. A Buick Skylark, not new. I can almost see her in the driver's seat, with one hand at the bottom of the steering wheel, kind of resting there the way she always drove, and the seat-belt strap pulled tight over her left shoulder. It's hot in the car and getting stuffier. There's an arc of beaded haze clouding up the rear window and getting bigger. Hanging down from the ignition key is the ring with the silver heart Byron and I gave her last Easter. The New York State inspection sticker's peeling on the windshield.

Outside the car it's completely dark. But still, Mom sees pinwheels and zigzags of light in front of the hood. The air's heavy and sweet, like up in the country, where the roads tunnel through the trees. It's like not being outdoors at all. There's the sudden light from fireflies and the glowing eyes of little animals crouching on the center stripe, hypnotized by surprise, until the last second when they make a run for the ditch.

I feel the tiredness creeping up on Mom, fogging her thoughts and her eyesight, making the dark brighter. She takes her hand off the wheel for a moment to scoop the strands of hair back from her forehead the way she always did when she was really worn out. I can see her slipping past thinking and maybe dreaming something meaningless, the way you do sometimes when you're really still awake. I can imagine her not having any pain or fear. Then between one moment and the next: nothing.

When Byron came home that night, I suppose he checked to see if I was in bed. I think I remember the door opening and closing. He usually made the rounds at night, looking for his cat, Nub, using this as a standard excuse to look in on me. Even though he knew I always threw Nub out of my room before I went to bed because he'd sleep on your face if he got the chance. Also Nub sometimes brought in a little tribute and left it on your pillow: a dead mouse, an exhausted roach, a moth missing its wings—something like that.

Grandmother came in about eleven as usual, though I was completely out by then and didn't hear her cane on the stairs. It was Mrs. Schermerhorn's chauffeur, Nathan, who found Mom early the next morning, the last day of April. He was out in the alley by six, wiping down the Cadillac with a KozaK cloth. Nathan's pretty much in charge of the alley, always going around to see that everybody's garbage can has a tight lid, and keeping a ring of all the garage keys for people who are always losing their own.

He must have seen our garage windows were fogged over. By then the Buick had run out of gas, so he wouldn't have heard the engine idling. Anyway, he must have worked through his ring of keys till he came to ours—he color-codes them. Then when he swung our garage door up he must have seen the hose running from the car's exhaust and snaking up into the wing window. He found Mom sitting upright in the front seat, where she'd killed herself.

I can picture Nathan jerking at the door handle and finding it locked. I can even see his old fist wrapped in the KozaK cloth shattering the driver's side window with one blow. His arm with the snow-white cuff turned back is angling inside through the broken star of glass to ease the door lock up. And then he yanks the door open, holding his breath against the carbon monoxide. He reaches out to Mom still held in place by the shoulder-strap seat belt, with her head resting back. I can see Nathan's hand reaching for Mom's wrist, even though he'd know there wasn't any life left in her.

Two

All the details of death on TV shows are lies. All those beautiful female mourners with short black skirts and great legs and dark glasses. All those silent Mercedeses winding through acid-green graveyards in a fine mist. The pin-striped undertakers. The organ music outdoors. And no real grief.

The night before Mom's funeral, friends are invited to call at Loring and Sons' funeral establishment in Manhattan, a high-rise mortuary with a different deceased on every level and people in the elevators calling out the names of the dead to be sure they get the right floor. In a way Loring's is a class act, not like the Brooklyn funeral parlors along Atlantic Avenue where you can see the body from the front door.

I spend most of two days feeling fairly numb, trying not to go too near myself, trying to keep

Byron in sight without hanging over him. But he isn't saying anything. And I don't know how to begin with him. He isn't doing anything either, and usually he's got a dozen projects lined up and going.

The guy in charge of the evening at Loring's has his own image: no pinstripes or white hands. He's trim looking, in a blue suit from Barney's, with wide lapels. I get weird vibrations off people that night. I think maybe he's just jogged over from a couple of fast tennis sets at the Grand Central Racquet Club. His hands are square, and he has a firm, dry handshake.

When we get there in Mrs. Schermerhorn's car, people are already signing the guest register. They stand around in knots ankle-deep in the carpet, glancing over at Grandmother and Mrs. Schermerhorn and Byron and me. Mom's coffin is between two floor lamps with torch-shaped glass shades. The lid's closed, according to Grandmother's instructions. Since there's nothing to see, people stay away from it. Grandmother's thought that through in advance.

All the heads in the room are half bowed. Some of the men hold their chins in their hands. The women brush things off their sleeves, and nobody speaks above a low hum. They hold back from coming over to us, nobody wanting to be first.

I watch how Grandmother grips the crook of her cane and tries not to lean on Mrs. Schermerhorn while they move very slowly across the room.

You don't second-guess Grandmother. I don't know what she's thinking. The biggest irony in the world must be to lose your own child, your only one. Maybe Grandmother thought she was the one who should be in that closed coffin. Maybe she thought there'd been some vast cosmic mix-up. And maybe there had. Whatever she was thinking, she was thinking it with a clear head. Dr. Painter had come around to the house that afternoon, bringing a bottle of Valium. But I don't think Grandmother took any. It's hard enough for her to accept a cane. She's not about to give in to a crutch.

Byron and I hang around the door while she and Mrs. Schermerhorn head for a sofa in the corner away from the coffin. Their heads are close together: Grandmother's nearly white, with every hair in place; Mrs. Schermerhorn's hair mahogany-dyed, springy and thin. Then Grandmother settles onto the sofa, giving her cane the usual little wrist action to scoot it behind her heels, where people won't fall over it or even notice it.

"Would you and your little brother like to . . . step up . . . nearer your mother?" I wonder if the undertaker in the Barney's suit is new on the job. He doesn't seem to have it together. I look down at Byron. It's a long way. I'm five eleven, practically, and he hasn't grown a quarter of an inch in six months. He's wearing a tie I knotted for him. No coat, and the tie's too long for him. It laps down over his fly. He doesn't seem to be noticing anything much, so I nod to the undertaker, and Byron and I walk down the center of the room to where Mom is. The undertaker keeps a half step behind us, and people make way.

When we get to the coffin it's like standing on the rim of a cliff. We've gone as far as we can go. Polished bronze, and a big spray of white rosebuds without a card or ribbon or anything. I think Grandmother asked Mrs. Schermerhorn to order the flowers. But there's nothing real about any of this scene.

Byron must be thinking the same thing. He speaks for the first time all day. I barely hear him. "Is she in there, Jim?"

I knew whenever he finally said something, I wouldn't be ready for it. "Yes, Mom's in there, in a way. In another way, she isn't."

"I don't mean the difference between the body and the soul," he says patiently. "I mean, is she cremated yet or not?"

"Not yet. Tomorrow, after the funeral."

I can feel people's eyes on us. Since our backs are to them, they're free to look. The dead woman's two sons paying their last respects. I never know what that saying means: paying your last respects. My hand automatically goes to my back pocket to see if I've remembered to bring my billfold.

This doesn't make any sense, so I think about trying to keep the communication open with Byron.

"She was dying anyway, By. You knew that. Nobody made a big secret of it."

"I know," he says. "She was hurting bad. Especially in the night."

I really need to cry now. A simple biological need. I'm too old just to stand there looking solemn like Byron. I have other—needs. I can't let him see me falling apart. Still, it's beginning to happen. SON COLLAPSES IN GRIEF ACROSS SUICIDE MOTHER'S COFFIN. Headlines blare inside my head. I can feel my face crumpling, from the chin up, and my throat closing. The undertaker's hand falls on my shoulder, resting there without pressure. And this nearly pushes me over the edge.

But help's on the way. The white rosebuds on Mom's coffin are beginning to run together when a woman steps up, invading the neutral circle around Byron and me. I can't be sure, but I think she waves the undertaker away. His hand leaves my shoulder.

"You're Jim Atwater?" she says. I look at her, blinking like crazy. Byron peers around me. She's familiar in a way, some friend of Mom's who used to drop in occasionally. Not anybody too close. I think once when Mom had just come from the hospital this woman stopped by and left a stack of magazines or something.

"Yes, I'm Jim. This is my brother, Byron."

"I'm Winifred Highsmith. I went to school with your mother. You know, Katharine Gibbs, the place where they taught us to wear white gloves and type."

Byron's giving her his total attention. Her voice has a cutting edge. But other people in the room start talking a little louder. Since somebody's made the first move toward Byron and me and the coffin, the decibel level rises.

She must be Mom's age: forty-six. She looks it. Tired New York eyes, jet-black hair pulled back tight, drawing her eyebrows up. She's nearly as tall as I am, and her eyes make contact with mine and won't let go. "I don't suppose they allow smoking in here."

"I don't know." My throat seems to be opening up again.

"It doesn't matter. It wouldn't help." She shifts the long strap of a purse higher on her shoulder. "Listen," she says, "I forgot you were going to be so grown-up. I never can keep track of people's children. One day they're wearing Pampers; the next day they're flunking out of college. You know what I mean?"

"Yeah, I think so."

"I'm not married. Never was. No kids. I always liked your mother." She talks in a jerky way, and her hand flips at the catch on her purse, going for a cigarette that wouldn't help, I guess. "I won't say all those things you're about to hear from other people. I'm rotten at that. I'll just talk a couple minutes and then leave. Okay?"

"Sure," I say. "That's—fine." I can see her clearer. My eyes aren't blurred. She looks kind of fierce.

"Where's your sister? Aren't there three of you?"

"She can't come. She's married and living in Germany. Her husband's in the Air Force."

"*Married?* Oh, well. I suppose I must have known that. What is she, about twenty?"

"Twenty-three."

"Ye gods."

"And she couldn't travel. She's pregnant."

"How far along?"

"Seventh month."

"So you and Byron will be uncles."

"Yeah. I hadn't thought about that. I guess we will."

"Let's see. Her name's Lorraine, right? Did she marry a nice guy?"

"Better not ask Grandmother, but yes, she did."

"Not up to the mark with Granny?" Winifred Highsmith runs her tongue along the inside of her cheek.

"Not quite. He's a sergeant, and Grandmother thought the least Lorraine could do was aim herself at the officer class." I'm beginning to forget we're standing two feet from my mother's coffin, from my mother. It's like a regular conversation. I'm probably even hanging too loose.

"Your mother wouldn't have given two hoots about that kind of thing. That's one of the things I liked about her. I suppose your father isn't here."

"He—he may be here tomorrow," I say fast, wanting to keep off the subject of Dad with a stranger while Byron's there at my elbow, all ears.

"Oh, yes." Winifred Highsmith rolls her eyes. "That's your father to a T. A dollar down and a day late, as they say."

"He'll probably be here," I say in a low voice, feeling stupid for trying to cover for him.

"But where was he when she needed him?" she says, looking fiercer. "How long was she sick—really sick? A year? Longer? Look, I'm sorry. Forget it. Howard's your father, and I should keep my big mouth shut. I never really knew the guy anyway. People's husbands—who can keep track?"

"I don't remember him that well myself. It's been about eight years or so since he left." It was exactly eight years. I know because Byron was only a baby at the time.

"You don't see him?" Winifred says.

"He lives down in Florida. It's a long way." There I go again, covering for this crumb.

"Yes," she says. "Hell of a long way. No planes, no phones, no word sent or received. Supplies sent in annually by native bearers. There, see? I can't keep still. Forget it, will you? Your mother was better off without him. Besides, she had you. Look, I've got to go now. I can take just so much of this type atmosphere. I came because I read about Barbara—your mother—in the *Times*. She was a great gal, you know what I mean? A little under your grandmother's thumb, if you know what I mean, but then who wouldn't be? And I really liked her—your mother, I mean. How many people do you really like in a lifetime?"

I shrug, not knowing. "Okay, I'm going to cut out now." She hitches the strap up on her shoulder again and opens the catch on her purse. "I'm truly not gifted at things like this. I probably won't see you again, either of you. I mean like day after tomorrow I'll pass you on the street, and you'll be married with five kids, and it'll be 1999. You know what I'm saying? I never can keep up with people's kids. You'll be fine now. In situa-

tions like this, it's getting through the first part
that counts. The trouble is, I never can stick it
out past that. Here come the rest of them."

Then she's gone, taking long strides across the
room. She has thick calves, like a dancer. And she
doesn't slow down going past Grandmother.

The rest of them move in, advancing on Byron
and me from three sides. My throat tenses up
again. But I can control it. Winifred Highsmith's way out in the hall now, waiting for the
elevator, fumbling in her purse. She's seen me, and
Byron, through the first, bad part. And it must
have cost her something. She never looked at
Mom's coffin. Maybe she couldn't.

The others surround us. I'm very bad with
names. Friends of Mom, and older people, friends
of Grandmother. Neighbors from Brooklyn
Heights: arty types, banker types. Grandmother's
entire Monday Evening Club, moving in under
the direction of Mr. Carlisle Kirby.

"Sorry," the men say, like they bumped you in
the subway. And handshakes. Quickies, lingerers,
grippers, wet fish, double-handed ones that put
your hand and your elbow in a vise. Mr. Carlisle
Kirby's knuckle-crusher to show what he has left
at the age of eighty. And the women who want to
say something appropriate about Mom, and something careful. All Brooklyn Heights knows how
she died. "You can keep anything here but a
secret," Mom used to say. And what Brooklyn
Heights knows spreads over the Bridge, infiltrates
Manhattan, Westchester, Bergen County, finally

ending up in the mental files of people who don't even know Mom firsthand.

The women cup Byron under the chin, try to pull him against them. They can barely keep from patting him on the head. He's taking it okay, but I want to punch them out. Then the tide ebbs, and I can begin to breathe again. The Monday Evening Club moves across toward Grandmother. I catch a glimpse of Mrs. Schermerhorn's hand touching Grandmother's arm to alert her. Grandmother's head comes up, ready to handle their sympathy. Then she's lost in a small sea of gray heads and lace handkerchiefs.

My best friend from school, Kit Klein, comes in then. His mother's with him. To keep my mind occupied, I try to figure the logistics of this. Did she come to make sure *he'd* come? Or did she tag along with him? I decide he's come on his own. And she's come not because she's pushy or morbid. They live over on Park Avenue, so it's no big pilgrimage. I begin to think about handling sympathy. Just take it, don't ask questions. Don't dissect.

"Listen, man, I'm really sorry," Kit says. He's wearing the school tie like I am, the only ties we own. Little wine-colored shields on a green silk background with gold daggers in between. They're symbols, but of what nobody knows. We're both wearing winter tweed sports coats. Kit's forehead is greasy. He's bigger than me, taller, wider across the shoulders, thicker in the neck. Wrestling team. "This is my mother," he says, remembering not to jerk a thumb at her.

My head goes a little haywire, and I nearly say, "And this is *my* mother." I even start to glance back at the coffin but catch myself.

"We're very sorry," Mrs. Klein says, shaking my hand. I introduce her to Byron, and she shakes his hand too, keeping her distance, no head patting. Then she steps back and melts into the crowd.

Byron gazes up at Kit and me. Whenever any of my friends are around, he thinks we own the world. Kit's stubbing his size twelve into the carpet, looking down into the pile for a clue to deal with this situation. He's a good friend, but we're not too verbal with each other. And he's working hard these days on self-improvement, which is a pretty solitary project.

"Working on my couth" is his phrase to explain away no longer calling girls chicks, owning a nail file, avoiding his all-time favorite two words: "tough shitsky," buying shirts with thirty-six-inch sleeve lengths to match his thirty-six-inch arms, going from a C-minus with warnings to a B-plus in English. He's starting to think seriously about Swarthmore, Wesleyan, and Williams, in that order, for year after next.

And this is the guy the entire school locker room gave a gift-wrapped can of Right Guard to as recently as ninth grade.

He thinks of something to say. "Your dad coming?"

From Kit this is okay, even with Byron there, drinking in every word. Kit's parents are divorced too. Half the guys at Van Cortlandt are from frac-

tured families. No need for fantasy fathers to keep
up your self-image.

"Yeah, tomorrow—maybe. Who knows? Grandmother had Mr. Kirby call him. I guess he said
he'd try to make it. But after eight years who
counts the minutes?"

Kit absorbs this, identifying probably. But it's
really a message I've aimed at Byron in case he's
counting on Dad to come. And in case Dad doesn't
come, which I expect. Maybe it'd be better if he
didn't show. I don't want Byron hassled.

"I could come," Kit says, sort of booming it
out too loud, "to the funeral in the morning. If
you want me to. I can get out of school. I only
got—have history and Spanish in the morning."

"It's Advanced Placement history," I say.
"You're just hanging on by your claws. Miss one
session and you're down the tube."

"Come on, man." We're both grinning now,
and then suddenly remembering where we are.

"No, don't come," I say. "I'll see you Monday." I glance down at Byron. "Or whenever I'm
back."

"Okay," Kit says. "I wasn't using this like—for
an excuse to get out of school or anything. You
know."

"I know. We're big boys now."

He stuffs his hands in his pockets and scratches
his legs, making coins and keys jingle. An old
habit, dying hard.

"I like your mother," I say. "She's . . ."

"Couth," Kit says.

They leave then. Mrs. Klein signs the guest

book. The ballpoint disappears completely into Kit's big paw when he signs after her. There's a little silk tassel on the end of the pen, and it hangs out over the back of his hand while he writes. I can see all this from way across the room.

The thing is, I can't see a few hours ahead to the next day. I can't see my dad.

Three

It's a long night in between. Grandmother's Monday Evening Club in full force comes back to the house with us. Almah's on duty. The silver urn's full of Sanka, and there's a long tray of toast points covered with melted cheese and parsley.

When Byron and I go up to bed, Nub's coiled on the landing with the tip of his tail sticking up between his paws. His yellow eyes are at half-mast, seeing and asleep. Byron heads off down the hall to his room. I rack my brain for something to say. "Good night" sounds too formal, too heavy. "You want me to help you get your tie off?"

"No, I can do it."

I stand in my room, slumped against the closed door, thinking about not falling apart in all this quiet. My room. Taller than it is wide, a hundred years old. Older than Mr. Carlisle Kirby, older than anybody in Brooklyn Heights. It still has

the trailing-vines-and-morning-glories wallpaper
somebody put up in World War I. The morn-
ing-glory purple and the vine green are merging
into one uniform khaki color. What was this room
set up for? Guests. Nobody permanent. I never
even thought of it as my room. It's the room I
got when Mom and Lorraine and Byron and I
came to live with Grandmother after Dad took a
walk. It's weird that none of us thought of doing
over a room to make it our own.

We were just passing through until . . . Dad
came back, or we got a place of our own, or I
don't know what. But Lorraine finished growing
up in one of these rooms, majored in Ed. Psych. at
Hunter for a few terms, and married an Air Force
sergeant she met at the counter at Chock full
o'Nuts. And Mom lived the rest of her life in a
guest room. Two guests down, and two to go.

I think about lying across the bed without un-
dressing, avoid this like a trap, then do it. The
minute I'm down on the bed, all I can think
about is Mom, like I'm her sole survivor. Two
nights ago she was sitting strapped in the front
seat of the Buick, undiscovered. Last night she was
on a marble slab, being drained. Tonight she's under a lid on Madison Avenue. Tomorrow night
she'll be ashes. Even the thing—the disease that was
growing in her—will be ashes. I can cry now in
total privacy. So let it happen. Nothing does.

I roll off the far side of the bed and head for
the bathroom, dry-mouthed, dry-eyed. Strip off
my clothes and put them on hangers on the back of
the door because these are tomorrow's uniform too.

I arrange the school tie around the crook of the hanger.

The shower's an even more private place. The big white square tiles are veined with millions of hairline surface cracks, the grout dried up into crumbling gray beads. The big steel shower head at the end of the gooseneck pipe is a mile high so you always have to wash your hair when you shower. I stand in there drowning while the water runs down between my legs. The tub fills knee-deep because the drainpipe's slow. The water's rusty-pipe brown, darkening as it deepens. It's like standing up to your kneecaps in hot tea. Then the breeze from the open window starts plastering the shower curtain against my side, and I can't get away from it. So I wrench the knobs shut, jerk the curtain aside, and step back into the world.

I don't plan on sleeping, but I'm asleep almost before I can crawl into bed, still damp inside my pajamas. Usually I don't wear anything to bed. But this is a special night. It calls for all kinds of respectful respectability and caution and protective covering. I sleep for four hours without moving my arm off my forehead.

And I dream. I'm back at Loring and Sons in the room with the coffin between the floor lamps. It's even worse than reality because this is a dream. The room's completely empty. Even Byron's not there. The guest register's lying open on the table by the door, completely filled up with signatures. The ballpoint with the tassel is out of ink. Everybody who's come to pay respects has

paid them and left. Everybody's paid but me. In
the dream it's exactly the hour I'm dreaming it—
two in the morning. And I've been left behind
and locked in the House of the Dead, and it's accurate down to details. Except for the walls. Instead of Loring's dull gold paint, there's a paper
patterned with faded vines and morning glories.

I step farther into the room. The lamps at either end of the coffin flicker like real torches.
With every move I make, the room gets smaller.
My feet sink into the carpet, but with each step
there's less floor. The ceiling's coming in too. It's
powered by some kind of hydraulic mechanism
that lowers it in programmed stages. Edgar Allan
Poe computerized. Finally I'm stooping in this
room, which is now no wider than a hallway and
closing in. There's no place to go except toward
the coffin. The shadows urge me toward it. In
dreams there's only one direction.

Then we have the first of two big surprises. The
coffin lid is open. So okay. I haven't had the complete course. My dues aren't paid because I
haven't looked at my mother's dead body. Let's get
this dream on the road, and then let's get it over
with.

Still, I can't quicken my pace, hurry anything.
My timing's off. I get slowly closer to the coffin,
which is yawning open. It's all buttoned-down
white leather on the underside of the lid, like car
upholstery. And now I'm close enough to put
both hands on the edge of the coffin. I do. I look
up once at the lowering ceiling, and then I look
down into the coffin.

And here's surprise number two. It's not Mom lying in there at all. It's somebody else. There's been a vast cosmic mistake. The entire dream changes mood. It's not even terrifying. It's too confusing.

There's a man lying there in Mom's coffin. I know he's dead. People often die with their eyes open. He's wearing a sports shirt. Ivory palm trees on a red background, open at the neck. Short sleeves, hairy arms, a big guy, completely filling up this woman-size coffin. I can see the rim of his teeth through slightly parted lips. This is not Loring and Sons' best work. He needs a shave, but he has a hell of a good tan.

And I can't just walk away and try another floor at Loring's. Because this particular corpse is my dad.

The knob on my bedroom door turns, and I'm awake and half out of bed. One heel hits the floor. I fight off the sheet. The digital clock says two-oh-seven and flips to eight. "Who is it?"

"Jim?"

"Nub's not in here, Byron."

"I know. He's still on the landing. . . . Can I come in?"

"Sure." The door opens wider, and there's a trapezoid of dim light on the floor. Byron's shadow fills part of it, elongated. Still, he doesn't come all the way in. I'm completely awake, glad to be out of the dream but I'm not sure what I've got here to deal with. "You want the light on?"

"I guess."

He's standing in the doorway, small hand still clenched over the knob. He's got this destroyed look on his face. This is natural, I tell myself. He's been too poker-faced up till now. I stare into this little kid's old face, looking for a sign. Then I see he's wearing pajama tops and a bathrobe and no pajama bottoms. Little white spindly legs disappear down into high-sided bedroom slippers. We stare at each other.

Finally he says, "I couldn't help it." His voice cracks in every direction. He's too upset to cry. Nobody at the age of eight should be too upset to cry. His chin keeps bucking back against his throat.

"You want to vomit?" I say, standing up.

"I want to, but I won't." And then it's breaking over me. He's embarrassed. I've seen this in him before, but not often, and I wasn't looking for it now.

"What happened? Come on over and sit down on the bed."

He pulls back, almost hides behind the door. "No. I—I woke up. And . . . I'd wet the bed." His face goes all out of shape. He's shamed himself and dirtied himself, and it's too much for him to handle. He doesn't see that it's part of the bigger thing—reaction. In a way it's almost a relief, at least to me. I walk over to him, and he cowers. I can't help it. I'm standing over him, and I'm enormous to him.

He's shaking his head and looking up, and I see

the whites of his eyes. "Why did I do it? I haven't done it since I was little. So why?"

"Look, it doesn't matter. Nothing that happens tonight or tomorrow counts. Just take my word for it." I've got my hand on his shoulder. It's like a bird's shoulder, full of webbed bones. "Listen to me, it doesn't count." I give him a shake for emphasis. "Come on, we'll change the bed."

"I don't know where the clean sheets are," he moans, and every word falls apart. If this kid could break down and cry, it'd be like a summer rain. I turn him around, and we walk down the hall to his room. Past Mom's room. Past Grandmother's. We won't be disturbing her sleep. I know that she's in there lying fully conscious with the unopened Valium bottle on her bedside table and her cane under the bed, at the ready, ready for morning. I know she hears us. And she knows I'm coping with Byron, while she's coping with herself.

He stops at the door of his room, suddenly doesn't want me in there. I reach over his head and run my hand down the wall for the switch. The overhead light clicks on. It's a regulation room for this particular house. Blistered wallpaper with some secret-code design, and an odd-lot selection of furniture featuring a brass bed. There's a sink in the room with a tacky square of linoleum under it. Some ancient homeowner's idea of a handy guest-room facility. Byron's pajama pants are wadded in the sink.

He's pulled the top sheet down off his bed. There's a big stain in the middle, already soaked in. No smell yet. I walk around him, very brisk. Big brother taking over. "Pull the sheet out at the bottom on your side," I say. We fold the sheet back, flip his pillow off on the floor. The same stain's on the quilted mattress cover underneath.

"Oh, no," Byron whispers.

"That's what mattress covers are for." I hope, when we get it off, the stain hasn't gone any deeper. "Reach under the mattress over there. The cover's attached with elastic across the corner." He heaves up the mattress, and the cover curls up. We fold it, and underneath on the flowered mattress there's a barely damp spot the size of a Frisbee. "That much won't matter," I say. "Get a wet washcloth."

I scrub away at the mattress, trying not to make a bigger wet place because Byron's fixated on it. "This'll dry," I say. "No harm done."

We find clean sheets out in the hall cupboard but no mattress cover. I lay a towel over the damp spot on the mattress and we make up the bed. I start to jam the sheets in on my side, but I notice Byron's squatting and making hospital corners on his side, the way Almah makes up our beds. So I pull my side free again, fold the corners into proper patterns. When we finish, the mattress looks like a gift-wrapped box.

I fold the stained sheets in on themselves, trying to make a bundle that's dry on the outside. "What'll we do with them?" Byron asks. "I don't want Almah to know."

"Forget about Almah," I say.

"She'll *find out*," he says. "She won't like it."

But we know that's not what he means. He doesn't want her to know or anybody to know that he's suddenly reverted to babyhood. He's eight years old, as old as he's ever been, and every minute of it should count in his favor.

Now it's all erased, and he's back at the beginning. I know exactly how it must feel, but I can't say so.

He hesitates by his bed directly under the hard light. If I tell him to, he'll crawl in and try to stay awake the rest of the night so he won't shame himself again. "Come on down to my room. Bring your pajama pants." I carry the bundle of sheets down the hall, and he follows. I tell him to take a shower in my bathroom. Then I start washing his pajama pants in my sink.

He gets into the shower and pulls the curtain across. Then he stuffs the robe and then the pajama top out over the edge of the tub, and they slip down on the floor. He's gotten suddenly modest lately. He showers a long time while I scrub away in the sink, doing a job on his pajamas with a nail brush and Irish Spring soap. I can see his outline through the plastic shower curtain. He's standing at attention under the shower, which is needling down on his head. He never raises his arms. He never shifts position. It's the shape of a little concrete gnome in a rock garden.

When he finally shuts the water off, I drop a towel over the top of the shower-curtain rod. Then I reach around and hand him his pajama top, then his robe. I wait until he pulls the curtain back and steps out of the tub, more or less fully dressed. It's almost funny, but I don't try to play it for laughs.

Instead, I'm standing there anticipating his next problem: what to do with the sheets. They're too messed up and wet to stuff in the hamper. I have a brainstorm and lead him back into my room. Then I hang one sheet out of each window. He watches this as if he's witnessing the invention of the wheel. "They go in the hamper in the morning."

"Almah will know," he says. "She counts everything."

I let this pass. "Get into bed," I say.

"Your bed?" His eyes are round. At rare moments his eyebrows almost meet in the middle. Now they're doing this.

"Sure."

"What if I—"

"You won't." I flip out the light.

It's not quite as wide as a double bed. We both shift around, trying to give the other as much room as there is. "I don't need a pillow," he says, pushing it my way. He needs a pillow more than anybody else I've ever known. He sleeps completely curled around one. I let him give me the pillow.

"Almah," he begins again, "she—"

"Byron, stop a minute and think, okay?" He lies there, suddenly mute. "Think about Almah if you want to. I mean really think about her. She's at home right now, down in Red Hook, right?"

"I guess so."

"She's worked for Grandmother for—I don't know how long. The beginning of time, right?"

"I guess so."

"And if Almah ever liked anybody in this whole family, it was Mom. Right?"

Silence. Then, "Yeah. She never said, but I think she liked Mom pretty much. When Mom was real sick, she'd stay late and do extra things."

"So how do you think Almah feels tonight?"

Byron lies there like a little mummy, wrapped in his robe, nose straight up toward the ceiling. He's giving this his complete consideration. "Bad?" he says finally.

"Really bad," I say. "Because she's the kind of person who can't show us how she feels, apart from complaining. I bet she's in her room down there in Red Hook staring at the walls."

There's a long silence then. If it was anybody but Byron, I'd think he'd gone to sleep. But then he says, "I know what you're saying. Almah's too upset right now not to be one of us, whether she wants to be or not."

"That's it."

"She might even be too upset to count the sheets," he says in a voice slipping toward sleep. That's all either of us knows till morning. When I wake up, Byron has my pillow, and it's tucked into his chin, and he's sleeping furiously into it.

Four

Fifteen minutes before the funeral, and something's already gone wrong. Mrs. Schermerhorn and Mr. Carlisle Kirby are fanning out from Grandmother. Mom's coffin has been removed. It's down in front of the pews. The white rosebuds on the lid are upstaged by all the "floral tributes" Grandmother expressly asked people not to send. Big salmon-pink spikes of gladioli, yellow, heavy-headed chrysanthemums, other things I can't name. There's even been a mutiny in Grandmother's own ranks because the Monday Evening Club's sent a spray of red, white, and blue carnations.

People are already beginning to come in, settling behind some invisible line along the rear pews. I'm fairly confident that my dad isn't going to show. He'd surely be here by now. I think I'd recognize him if he were here. Haven't I just seen him a few hours ago wearing a sports shirt in Mom's coffin?

Mr. Kirby is having words with the undertaker, then three undertakers. His long, blue-veined hands are working in the air. His crooked finger's going to start tapping an undertaker's vest button any minute now. Artificial stained-glass daylight is striking sparks off his old bald head. The white fuzz growing out of his ears is quivering. He looks like an Old Testament prophet in a Brooks Brothers suit. And the undertakers are listening to him.

The problem is they've slotted us into exactly the chapel Grandmother didn't want. And she knows them all. There's no side room or curtained alcove for the family to sit in during the service. We're expected to sit down front in full view.

"Do I need to remind you people this is a *funeral*, not a wedding?" Mr. Kirby's outraged whisper carries all over the chapel. The undertakers are trying to hold their ground. "Do you people actually expect Mrs. Livingston and her family to sit out front, exposed to public scrutiny?" His whisper drops lower and gets more vicious. "Do you people *realize* how this looks?"

This could be bad for Loring and Sons' business. This is what Mr. Kirby means. His arm sweeps over the Monday Evening Club now taking up a complete pew, end to end. He doesn't actually have to spell out that they're all candidates for Loring and Sons' services in the near future.

The undertakers are computing this, letting Mr. Kirby have his say because they have no choice and because they haven't figured a way out of this yet. They aren't used to dealing with old men. They're used to burying old men. It occurs to them that Mrs. Livingston, Grandmother, has her own linebacker. He looks like Don Quixote, but he's got the impulses of a Wall Street lawyer who never admitted to retirement. He keeps going for the jugular.

But this is rush hour at Loring's. Every chapel is going full blast. A compromise is worked out. Screens are brought in on rollers, like the screens around Mom's bed when she was in the hospital ten, fifteen times. Mom still hasn't made her escape from all that yet—another hour to go. Even the flowers smell like a hospital room.

The screens are overlapped to make a little roofless room for us down front. This slows the countdown. Clocks stop. It's ten minutes after the hour before the organ begins to play, automatically, "Evening Star" from *Tannhäuser*.

Grandmother's not going to put herself on display. That's out. And she's trying to screen out what she can't foresee. She hasn't had a word with me about Mom's death. And she's kept even farther from Byron. How can she know how her grandsons will react? What if we disgrace her? She's depending on me to keep that from happening. But she likes a second line of defense. Is she worried about breaking down herself? No.

We're all rounded up and led down to the screens by undertakers moving like this was their own idea. They've left two empty folding chairs beside Grandmother, and they shepherd Byron and me toward them. But Grandmother pulls Mrs. Schermerhorn down on one side of her and motions Mr. Kirby into the seat on her other side. She's covered her flanks. Byron and I move into the row behind.

Grandmother's Dr. Painter is assigned an end chair in the enclosure. She'll show him what he can do with his Valium. One of Mom's doctors is there too. Grandmother knows how to show people their own limitations.

One of her distant cousins is in the doctors' row behind us, given a place because she's ridden the bus all the way down from Utica and deserves something. I don't know her name.

The service begins, conducted by a Congregational minister probably picked out of the Yellow Pages. Grandmother wouldn't have her own Episcopalian priest officiating. Would this be putting him on the spot because Mom was a suicide? I don't want to know the answer. Theology is not my thing. Byron sits silent and upright. His necktie falls in folds halfway to his knees over his clenched legs.

The sermon's in third person, with long Biblical quotations that bypass death and linger over the geography of the Holy Land. Sheep grazing on green hillsides above domed towns.

It's not hard to take, so I let my guard down and conduct my own service without benefit of clergy. She was dying anyway. A long, no-win, no-known-cure sentence of death. They couldn't even give her a set number of months. That's only on TV—daytime TV at that.

Only four lines, and he's kept his voice bland, no stage business. Mrs. Schermerhorn's hand remains unmoving within reach of her purse. Is this a prayer, or isn't it? Her hand seems unsure, even through the glove. Grandmother's head is still bowed.

Nothing is here for tears. But they're there anyway, setting little fires under my eyelids. *No weakness, no contempt, Dispraise, or blame.* No, no blame. She was dying anyway.

A death so noble. What are we supposed to do with this? Noble—to leave Byron and me? He's only a kid. Every day matters with him. He'd already been left by one parent. One he doesn't remember and now one he does—two quick jabs to the groin, both times when he wasn't looking.

No, that's the wrong direction; take another. Noble—not to let us see her turn into a vegetable shriveled with pain. Is this better? No, it goes nowhere. I can't buy it. Put that last line together and run it by again. *And what may quiet us in a death so noble.* I've got a handle on it now. The minister can call Mom's death noble because he doesn't even know how it happened. He's the only stranger in the room. But he's the one at the microphone. Later the rest will find their voices: poor Mom, poor Grandmother, poor sons, poor daughter way off in Germany, a shame, *the* shame. But right now we're all being purified by poetry, and silenced. So Grandmother knew what she was doing.

It's over, with no filing past the coffin, no pallbearers. Feet shuffle outside the screen. Grand-

mother waits until these outsiders realize we're
not coming out to be sympathized with again.
Then Mr. Kirby stoops for Grandmother's cane,
puts it in her hand. We stand up: the two of them,
Mrs. Schermerhorn, behind us the two doctors and
the cousin from Utica, Byron and I. The eight of
us.

No. Nine. Somebody's slipped in late, next to
the cousin. A stocky guy, my height. Blondish
hair going a little white at the temples. Rumpled
Palm Beach suit, narrow lapels, narrow tie, a shirt
collar point caught on the outside of the lapel.
Probably a one-suit man. Winging out from his
eyes are deep creases paler than his tan.

Grandmother pivots on her cane, ready to leave.
She catches sight of him, and it throws her timing
off, no more than a second. Mrs. Schermerhorn's
eyes dart back and forth.

"Well, Howard," Grandmother says to the
stranger, "these are your sons, in case you don't
know them."

Riding backwards on the jump seat in Mrs.
Schermerhorn's Cadillac, I watch the grille of the
Lincoln limo from Loring's tailing us. Across
town, around the lethal approach to the F.D.R.
Drive, gaining a little measured speed down past
Sutton Place and through the U.N. tunnel. Past the
helicopter pad and then curving out toward the
East River between Stuyvesant Town and the tennis courts, under the graffiti on the pedestrian
overpass. The tugboats are plugging along on our
level, curling the foam with their bows.

I watch the grinning grille on the Lincoln between Grandmother's face and Mrs. Schermerhorn's. Byron's glued to it too. The limo windshield's a mirror, beginning to reflect the Wall Street skyline. Behind it is the Loring driver and behind him Dad. Nothing real about this. It's only—traffic.

In our car absolute silence. Mrs. Schermerhorn's there because she knows not to fill up awkward silence with awkward chitchat. With Grandmother in the back seat, it's easy to forget this is Mrs. Schermerhorn's car. Grandmother's face is set. But upon what I don't know. Her plans haven't gone completely out the window. Right now we're into her alternate maneuver. She hasn't counted on Dad showing, but since he has, she can cover this too. No curbside rejections. No scene of any kind. He's to come back to the house for the funeral lunch, break bread with the sons he dumped. Squirm under the pitiless eye of his ex-mother-in-law. Pay.

The Fleetwood's tires hit the metal mesh on the Brooklyn Bridge. The bracing cables of the bridge flash past and ripple the Lincoln's hood behind us. We're still being tailed. Lose them, Nathan, step on it. Let's see what this old Fleetwood can do if you open her out for once.

Nathan brakes gently, and we take the first exit off the bridge, spiraling down toward Cadman Plaza. We swing into Montague Street, double back toward the river. Nathan hauls on the wheel. The Fleetwood steers like a semi. Two more sharp lefts, and we're home. We take up both parking spaces in front of the house. The Lincoln idles in the traffic lane, blinkers flashing. Nathan hands Grandmother and Mrs. Schermerhorn out. They wobble on the sidewalk, find their land legs. The sunlight turns the Lucite cane into a fiery rod. Before I can unfold my legs and get out of the car, Byron's hand is bunching my coat sleeve.

"Is that really Dad?" he whispers. "Ours?"

Almah's sister comes in to help serve the lunch. Rustling black shiny uniforms, Earth shoes, white aprons, no frills. Almah's face is a sculpture, carved with primitive tools. She has a jaw whittled out of some incredibly hard wood. Eyes that can spot trouble at tremendous range. Her sister tries to keep behind her at all times.

We don't fill up all the space, even when the whole Monday Evening Club reassembles. The average age now gathered together comes in at about seventy years, even figuring Byron and me in. And Dad. There's a knot of people in the front room, between the bay window and the Bechstein grand piano. Another couple of groups cluster in the windowless middle room, being stared down on by the portrait of my dead grandfather, looking like J. P. Morgan. The back room, always called "the summer dining room"—year around— looks down to the back of the garage wall across the garden. The buffet table's set up in there, still bare. All the flowers that have been sent to the house are down in the cellar, beginning to die of thirst.

People stand, then sit in isolated clumps with

distances between. It's the configuration of a subway car. There's an understanding that Grandmother isn't going to play hostess. She sits in the wing chair under Grandfather. Almah backs through the kitchen door with a tray of pre-poured sherry and two tumblers of milk. One milk for Byron, the other's for Mr. Kirby's ulcer. It's having a workout. He's on his feet but wavering, tall and hunched, in the middle of the middle room, halfway between Grandmother and Dad, who's barely inside the hall doorway.

I start walking through a lot of manufactured conversation toward Dad. He's not drinking the sherry. He's looking around the room, but he knows I'm getting closer. I remember Winifred Highsmith: "I never can keep track of people's children." "I'm Jim," I say to him, to Dad.

"Yes, I know. I had time to—work that out. I was sitting behind you. At the funeral." I wonder if our voices sound alike. You can never really hear your own voice, not even on tape. You're too occupied in thinking it isn't an accurate reproduction. I decide our voices are nothing alike. And his hair's a couple of shades lighter than mine, except it's got some white in it. We're not even built the same. Except I'm not forty-six.

"I'm seventeen." Should I say "*sir*"? Too stiff, almost a sneer. Nothing's right, but I didn't walk across this room to freeze him out. Why did I walk across this room?

"Seventeen last February," Dad says. It's eerie, annoying. Like having your palm read by a stranger who's a lucky guesser. "You were born in

Barnes Hospital, during a snowstorm. The only blizzard they'd had in St. Louis for years. We drove in as far as Clayton without snow tires, then got a cab somehow the rest of the way. But you took your time. You weren't born till the next day."

This is starting a ridiculously long way back to lay the foundations. But safe. "I didn't know that," I say. "I knew I was born in St. Louis. I have to put that down on forms for school. But I didn't know about the blizzard." We stand there looking at each other. I think I can read his mind. Shall we go on with this, recounting where and how Lorraine and Byron were born? We could fill up a lot of time this way. We were all three born in different places while Dad was moving around, climbing the corporate ladder of some company. That was before he fell off the ladder, or jumped. I see by his face that calling the roll of births isn't the way to go.

It occurs to me that the reason there's nothing familiar about him is that (a) I was nine when he left and so he looks shorter now, and (b) I've never seen a picture of him. He got erased from the family.

"Lorraine's in Germany," I say. "She's married."

"I know. There are always people who tell you things." He doesn't say who these people are, how the network for information works. It sounds complicated, spotty. "What are you thinking?" he says, catching me well off base.

"I don't know," I say. "I'm just taking every word as it comes. They're not exactly flowing."

"I was thinking about the first time I was ever in this room," he says. His eyes moved around, skipping over Grandmother. "I followed your mother home one day. Nine hundred miles. We were both still in college. I met her at this resort in Saugatuck, Michigan. I washed dishes—ran the dishwashing machine. Barbara—your mother— worked in registration."

The conversation keeps spiraling back in time. He'll be back to his own birth at this rate.

"I think I must have been just about as uncomfortable that first time here as I am now. Some things never change. You never really grow up."

This line is too easy. I let it pass. It's creeping up on me that this guy has not turned up after an eight-year coffee break ready with excuses and a smoke screen of big talk. I was expecting something a little more overbearing. His eyes still roam around the rooms. There's a pointlessly big chande- lier in the middle of the ceiling. A denim bag was put around it in preparation for summer. But Al- mah took the bag off early in the morning, and Nathan came over to help. Dad looks at it, and then his gaze drops to a point behind my shoulder, where Grandmother's sitting.

"Still a lot of starch in her upper lip," he says.

Almah and her sister are bringing the food into the summer dining room. Almah's carrying a long tray of chicken-salad sandwiches—it's always chicken salad—and the tray isn't buckling under the weight. Her sister's struggling with the Sanka urn. I think about rounding up Byron. But I don't see him. Mr. Kirby's milk glass is still in his hand. The other glass, drained, is on the piano.

"I've got to go find my brother," I say, ready to walk around Dad. Where's Byron? I don't want him left alone. I let him out of my sight for one minute, and he—

"Can I help you look?" Dad says.

"No." I'm at the foot of the stairs. And I wait long enough to keep Dad from falling in behind me. Then I head up.

Byron's in his room, hanging around by the front window, but not looking out. The light's tricky in there, north light bouncing off the brownstone fronts across Remsen Street. It's a moody, late-afternoon kind of room. He's got one hand on the sink. I wonder if he's been sick. The bed we made up so neatly in the middle of the night is still tight and untouched.

"What are you doing up here?"

He looks up, and the light halos all around his slicked-down hair. "I didn't know where else to *be*," he says in a strangled voice. "So I just came up here. Where was I supposed to *be*? You didn't want me talking to *him*, did you?"

Probably I didn't. Big brother runs interference. Big brother moves out first from base camp, checking unknown terrain. Big brother checks swamp for deadly quicksand. "Come on," I say. "It's time for lunch. Get washed up. Roll up your sleeves. You didn't eat much breakfast. You're probably hungry."

Byron's eyes flick away from me, to the door.

Dad's standing in it. I don't know what I feel about this. Not a regular kind of anger.

"Is he all right?" Dad says, practically whispering. He doesn't know this little kid. He hasn't made the contact. I'm standing there between them. I point at the sink, and Byron reaches for the soap. Don't try to walk around me to get to him. But Dad doesn't try. "Can I see your room?" he says.

"What for?"

"I'm in no hurry for the chicken salad?" he says. "I never was."

I lead him away from Byron back through the length of the house, open my door, and let him walk in. "My God," he says, "the same wallpaper." He scans all the morning glories and vines. I wonder what he was expecting. Pennants from all the Ivy League schools? Punk rock posters? Complete collection of vintage beer cans?

"This was the room I stayed in that first time," he says. "I had the distinct impression that Grace—your grandmother—sat out in the hall all night with a musket across her knees."

One more cheap shot at Grandmother, and I'm either going to come to her defense or defect to his side. Why this is turning out to be the big moral issue of the day amazes me.

But Dad walks across to one of the rear windows, looks down at the garden and the tar roof of the garage. He stands there with his hands locked behind him, wrinkling up his coat. Byron stands that way sometimes, like a little old man.

We can't keep things on this level, I think.

Not through lunch. It's a no-man's-land, nothing clear-cut. And nobody's going to take him off my hands. I move up behind him. He's still looking down through the dogwood branches in full flower.

"That's where she died," I say. "Mom."

"In the garden?" He turns on me, this astonished look on his face.

"No. In the garage."

"In the *garage?* What are you talking about?" His hand comes up to grip my arm. But we haven't touched, and don't. There's a wall there. "How in the hell did that happen? Didn't she die of . . . Wasn't she in the hospital when . . ." His voice trails off, but he's waiting for an explanation. And I see now he needs one. It was Mr. Kirby who called Florida to tell him Mom died. That's all he told him.

"Mom killed herself. In her car."

And then Dad's face goes all out of shape. He has this destroyed look. Byron gets it sometimes.

Five

Monday morning. Dad's gone back to darkest Florida, leaving no trace. And no Final Words; at least he had one thing in common with Mom. I come down dressed for school in case I'm going.

I'm going. It's written all over the dining-room table. The table groans with routine, business-as-usual, Grandmother's not downstairs; she never is for breakfast. Byron gets up an hour later since he only has to walk around two corners to get to his school, Brooklyn Heights Collegiate. We're both going to school. Two hot-cereal bowls are set out. Oatmeal till the last day of school even if there's a killer heat wave, even if there's a recession in rolled oats. Almah's making stirring noises in the kitchen.

There's an airmail letter from Lorraine—weepy, suffering. I can't get through it, set it aside, turn to the next item. The application for a summer

camp counseling job I mislaid somewhere has
made a comeback by my juice glass. Grandmother's hand at work the night before. What do
we have here? Name, age, previous camp experience, major sports, sports qualified to coach, water-
front skills, other talents please list for example
story-telling, auto mechanics, dramatics, crafts,
musical instruments, woodworking, specify
power-tool proficiency. References. Five dotted
lines for biographical sketch.

Tell us your hopes, your heartbreaks, your nas-
tiest vices, and the college of your choice, and
maybe we'll pay you a hundred a month to teach
twelve-year-olds beadwork when they'd rather be
drag racing.

There's also a pile of literature beside Byron's
place. I read brochures upside down, topped with
*A Parents' Guide to Outdoor Summer Experience
in the Tri-State Area.* Separate folders for camps
in Connecticut, Upstate, the Ramapos. We're going to get through the next few weeks somehow,
and then we're going to be packed off. The summer's as far ahead as even Grandmother can see. I
don't see much past it myself. Another year and
four months, make that sixteen months, and I'll be
ready for college. But I can't see that far, and
where does that leave Byron?

But back to the present. Have I got a prayer of
landing a camp job this late, even Camp Candle-
wood in Boondock, Vermont? Yes. Mr. Carlisle
Kirby is on the camp board. I'm a shoo-in. The
place on the application for references has been x-
ed out for my convenience. The Gray Panthers

strike again. The elderly can't deal with you, but they sure as hell can deal in your behalf.

Even as I shuffle through the application form, Mr. Kirby is gearing up for Mom's inquest, drawing in Grandmother's lawyer so he won't feel out of it. He puts his own lawyer on call, ready to coach Nathan if his evidence is challenged or if Authority leans on him. The Family is to be spared all known hassles.

I don't know all this at the breakfast table. It leaks out in dribbles over the next month, even after the inquest is a . . . dead issue. You hear things in an old house. The walls talk. Stairwells echo. Even the closed door of Mom's room mutters. A word here and there wafts up from the middle parlor when the Monday Evening Club's in session. Mr. Kirby uses our phone, which, weirdly enough, is built into an ancient phone booth under the stairs in the hall. Mr. Kirby speaks in a carrying voice because he's slightly deaf and doesn't know it.

I learn nothing from Grandmother. Zero. Even if I wanted to, there isn't enough curiosity in the world to breach her defense. Inquest, coroner, suicide, even death itself are not in her working vocabulary. And she wasn't put on this earth to be interrogated by a teenager. Or anybody else. Byron seems to have been born knowing this, and more, about her. But I have to keep relearning. On the subject of Grandmother, I'm remedial.

That first school morning I think her walls will never crumble. They will, but I don't know this yet. Life sends you damned few advance warnings.

Almah brings in the oatmeal, ladles it from a great height into the bowl. No raisins involved in these plops, not at a dollar twenty-nine a pound. We run a tight ship here. I hear Almah thinking. This is the fifth morning she hasn't had a breakfast tray to make up for Mom. There's still a hole gaping in Almah's day.

The subway stinks worse than usual. I'm in the front car where the same six girls are already on, talking around each other down the long seat. Why don't they ever talk to the ones nearest them? Their hair whips as they crane out past each other, firing conversation down the row. They go to some school that doesn't require uniforms, always leaping up in a bunch and exploding out the door at 72nd Street and ganging across to the local.

We've practically grown up together in the front car. But I don't know them. I only know strategic parts. They wear sandals today, and the one they always talk around paints her toenails purple-red. What is this? Compensation for being the group dodo?

All their skirts are too long and getting longer. I've committed their thighs to memory, but memory begins to blur. One girl doesn't shave her legs, almost doesn't need to. Peach fuzz, no bristles. How would Kit Klein in his uncouth days describe these legs? If skirts get any longer, I'll end up ankle-peeking like Mr. Carlisle Kirby in his youth.

We stop dead center in the middle of the East River tunnel. Complete power loss. Dead, underwater silence. The lights dim. Oceangoing vessels pass directly over our heads. Green Mafia corpses, scientifically weighted, graze the tunnel top with seaweed hands. Rats glance out from tile chinks at the sudden stillness of us becalmed underwater.

Then there's a bone-rattling take-off. Zilch to twenty miles an hour. The girls shriek. Notebooks slide from lap to lap. Knapsacks keel over. We're still going to school, won't even be late. They groan, roll their eyes. Even look my way. Small disasters permit this. But I keep their looks, don't even give them back. Inmates of boys' schools are misers by nature, who save such encounters to feed their fantasies in closed-door nights.

School's a blur, already winding slowly down to end-of-the-year. Kit Klein appears down a hallway, head and shoulders above the crowd. Sends out various types of hand signs to me. The general meaning being, you okay? Got through it all right? Great, see you later.

Mrs. Berger in English is especially gentle. We've been doing poetry. She'll give me the mimeographed sheets I missed. Everybody else turned in his paper on Modern-American-novel-of-year-choice Friday, but of course I can take my time handing mine in.

"Tomorrow," I tell her. She's looking up from her desk at me, through a haze of black hair, silent sympathy sent out in microwaves.

"Take your time," she says again, softly. Her breasts are a major handicap. Big-breasted women who teach in boys' schools have to struggle for eye contact. Some of her students have never seen her face. She has a fantastic wardrobe of high-necked blouses, loose jackets, bows under the chin. Nothing works. "What a pair," Kit Klein still says even in the pursuit of couth. "What a pair . . . va . . . va . . . va . . . VOOOM!"

I pass on from Mrs. Berger to trig, Contemporary Social Issues, chem, gym. Somehow it's Friday, then Monday again. For the first time I actually comprehend that routine isn't all bad. It sees you through. Bells ring and you move. Bells stop ringing and you sit down. The little guys I coach have their own way of handling me. They can't deal with death, so they don't mention it. And then they forget. We convoy across Broadway, into the park. The usual squabbles break out.

They get worse as we near the end of school. After all, we're the Van Cortlandt Academy farm team, perpetually in spring training for a season that never comes. These are not the Boys of Summer. We'll never play Shea. And they don't honestly believe they'll ever be upper schoolers qualifying for the Real Team. I'm their only link with this Big Time. Upper schoolers, even me, are Supermen, have the world wired. Able to knock the ball out of the park, out of the Bronx, out of the solar system. So they wait hopelessly and listen restlessly while little Ricky Hatfield, clown of fifth grade, does his Howard Cosell imitation for the millionth time, and then they resume squabbling.

We train less, exercise less, worry about finesse

less, and play more ball. When we're up to strength, we can just field two teams. With our own rules. Giants and Dwarfs, by name, which has nothing to do with comparative heights. There are giants and dwarfs on both teams, evenly divided by me. There's no grabbing up a bat handle to choose players: this creates rejects, and I don't want any water boys.

Our own rules are strictly our own. If the Giants get a double and a single and still don't score, while the Dwarfs get only two singles and don't score, the Giants win. And vice versa. No overtime. Mysteriously, the floodlights stop going on, possibly to honor late daylight, possibly to honor Con Ed.

They like our private variations in the rules. It sets them apart, makes them more clubby, and boosts morale until they can get to their various summer camps. Then they can lie like bandits about this great school team they star in.

I come home one night fairly late, stopping off first at Burger King. We don't pretend to have family meals any more. This goes back to Mom's sickest days. Almah gets Byron fed before she goes home, and that's all Grandmother or I care about. I've lost some weight since Mom died, and I don't have any to lose. Besides, the annoying headlines are blaring in my head again. SUICIDE'S SON PINING AT SENSELESS LOSS EXPIRES OF HUNGER. I come home carrying a second chocolate shake, double thick.

The front hall light's off, and I hit the stairs at my usual top speed. I nearly run Grandmother down. I actually bump into her, our first human contact in years, maybe ever. Her cane clatters against the banister. We grab each other. Somehow she keeps her cane, and I keep my chocolate shake. Two other people would get a laugh out of this. All we get is a sharp intake of breath. We're all tangled up. I step down a step, see that she isn't going to topple forward. I can't tell if she'd been heading up or coming down.

Then I begin to see. She's been standing there in the gloom, waiting for me. It's true we have a lot to discuss, now that Mom's no longer there in between us. Like, where do we go from here? After the summer, after we start crawling out of our post-funeral shells into our normal-size larger shells. But redefining relationships with Grandmother? Getting it all together with Granny? I can't see it. It's science fiction. So what are we on the brink of?

I wait while she pulls herself together. The cane shifts from hand to hand, one grip on it, the other on the railing. "Jim, I thought you'd better know. Nathan was good enough to sell it for me."

Her voice is weak and strong at the same time. But what's she talking about? "He took it someplace out on Northern Boulevard. And he received seven hundred dollars for it. I wanted him to take something for . . . all his trouble, but of course he wouldn't hear of it." Her voice gathers strength at Nathan's strength of character, which is already well known. She's giving my slow boy-brain time to know what she means without having to spell . . . it . . . out. Northern Boulevard, in Queens:

used car territory. Nathan's sold Mom's Buick Skylark. I have a quick flash of him easing into the seat where Mom died and nosing the Death Car up the Brooklyn-Queens Expressway ramp.

"—a good price for it, I think."

Her cool is half shot if she's talking money. Money is another of her taboo topics. But she knows I haven't been near the garage, won't go. And she thinks I better know what's happening. You can talk about a car, even this one, with a boy because cars belong to the man's-world category of points, plugs, buying, selling, trading off.

She's still speaking, in starts and stops. "—divided equally between your savings account and Byron's."

This is our entire inheritance, though she doesn't lay this on me. We've lived off her for years. And all the hospital bills "threatened her capital," in Mr. Kirby's crisp, money-crackling phrase that floated up the stairwell more than once.

This is it then. She wants me to know the car's sold. Period. Not even any heavy advice about keeping my half of the take untouched in savings. I could draw out my entire three hundred and fifty dollars on the day of deposit and blow it, and she'd never seem to know. Because if she starts trying to raise us, she'll be committed. We're orphans now in her eyes. Dad never counted. Orphans need care, but cars can be sold. I understand this. I'm glad the car's gone in case I ever have to go out to the garage.

She's heading downstairs now, I see. Moving around me with impatient little twitches of her cane, all her hurt nicely bottled up except for that unconscious wrist action on the cane's crook.

We may not find anything to say again for days. So over my shoulder I say, "Nathan got a good price for it."

She observes a moment of silence. Then, "Well, I wouldn't know. I would simply assume."

The next day I get called out of Contemporary Social Issues, last period of the day. There's been a phone message for me. The school office is having a tense moment. Secretaries' eyes fall on me and slew away. Trouble brewing, already brewed. What in the hell have I got left to lose? There's been a call either from Grandmother or Long Island College Hospital. And I'm supposed to go either there or home. We're not sure about this. I'm supposed to do something right away. The head secretary is giving me this garbled message from her shorthand pad. Her shorthand is perfection; it's the message that's giving her trouble. Even the punch line: my little brother is either dead or not. This point is not clear.

RICHARD PECK

came all her hair neatly brushed up under, for the
hospital. By when she got there I was more
wouldn't know. I would simply assume.

The next day I got called out of C

Six

Byron isn't dead. He's got to be hurting, though,
propped up like a stuffed owl against a hospital
pillow. Some numskull of a nurse has brushed his
hair up into a peak. I don't draw his attention to
it by flattening it down. But my hand aches to go
for my comb. Byron's right arm is in a sling, making an acute angle. Bandages run over his shoulder,
partway up his neck, and in the other direction
around his rib cage. He's trussed up and probably
itching. I don't know what kind of medication is
keeping him this calm. Maybe none.

This is the morning of the second day. I never
exactly sorted out the first day. The message, it
turns out, came from Grandmother *at* the hospital.
And Byron was in the emergency room, not the
morgue. Nobody actually mentioned morgue, but
on the West Side IRT downtown express I have

sharp impressions of cold slabs and clanging metal drawers. I am in a bad way.

When I get to the hospital that first day, Mrs. Schermerhorn's Cadillac is parked in the "Ambulance Only" zone. But Nathan's already taken Grandmother home and has come back, bringing Mr. Kirby and waiting for Mrs. Schermerhorn. They've already set up their routine. Dammit, you've got to hand it to those Gray Panthers.

Byron has maybe five blocks to walk home from school. He walks halfway with his buddy, Tim Somers, who cuts off down Garden Place. So we're talking about two and a half blocks alone. He doesn't make it on this particular afternoon. At the Joralemon–Henry Street intersection he's mugged by a gang. They pile out of an old Chevy without plates, driven by an older gang member who may or may not be the honcho. They wipe the crosswalk with Byron. Stomp him. Slap him around. Take his billfold. Shake him down. Then when they've picked him clean of a dollar and change, they kick him flat in the middle of the street, briefly blocking traffic. And some hero gives his arm an extra twist which in some freak way breaks his collarbone. "Right clavicle," to quote Blue Cross/Blue Shield.

Plenty of witnesses, of course. This is New York. A woman carrying a baby and a bag from Key Food somehow gets him out of the street after the Chevy tools off. The doorman of some building calls an ambulance, which takes its time. But nobody sees anything. This is New York.

The head night nurse, who pretends to speak no

English, puts me bodily out at the end of visiting hours. But I'm back the next morning. The academic life of Van Cortlandt Academy can struggle along without me. Likewise the Giants and Dwarfs. Let them think I'm having a delayed reaction to Mom's death. In a weird way I am. This is hitting me harder. I'm less numb, but that's only part of it. I'm feeling this more, and I'm not even guilty about my priorities. Even when I see Byron sitting up in the morning, coolly examining the sling like it isn't even on his arm. He has unbelievable detachment.

I try to read his eyes—a pointless habit of mine. *Where were you when I needed you?* No, I don't see that. It doesn't figure anyway. You shouldn't have to walk an eight-year-old kid home from school. On the other hand, that may be the only way to get him home alive.

"How's it going?" I say for a brilliant opener.

"It's broken," he says, sounding impressed.

"I meant—how's it going generally? You feel okay?"

"They have oatmeal for breakfast here too," he says. This is when I itch to smooth down his hair. In another way, I'm afraid to touch him. His unwrapped shoulder is just this small white mound, half hanging out of the ridiculous night-shirt thing they've got him wearing.

"You sleep any?"

He nods. I'm glad he doesn't ask me the same.

"Want to talk?"

"What about?"

Hell, I don't know. Who do you like in the

All-Star Game? Read any good books lately? What do you want to be if they let you grow up? "About what happened."

"I don't want to talk about that," he says, shaking his head. "Definitely not."

"Don't you want them to catch those . . . turkeys? Don't you want—" "Justice" is what I'm trying to say. But how do you ask an eight-year-old kid if he wants justice? Particularly when there isn't much of it around.

"I don't want to talk about it to *anybody*," Byron says. His head never stops shaking. "Come closer, and I'll tell you why." My knees are already nudging his bed. He wants me to lean over so he can whisper. He doesn't know if there's somebody in the bed on the other side of the curtain or not. There isn't. Even so, he wants to whisper.

"There were girls with them. In the gang." He lays his one small workable hand on the sheet and stares at it, while I think this over.

"Girls?"

"Yeah. It was a girl who took my billfold. I think it was a girl who stood on my back too. When they grabbed my arm and—"

"Okay. You don't have to go through it." Who am I trying to spare here—him or me? He has heel-mark lacerations on his back which I haven't seen yet. I'm still not getting his meaning, and he's a little exasperated about how thick my head is.

"I don't want anybody knowing girls were in

on it. How'd you like it if people said *you* got mugged by girls?"

Macho in the third grade. I can't believe it. "But there were girls *and* guys, weren't there?"

He nods. "But when people start talking, pretty soon it'll be girls only. Anyway, I couldn't identify them. And what if I could? They wouldn't do anything to them. They'd probably all be in Juvenile Court, which is nothing. Except maybe the driver, and he never touched me."

Oh, Lord, he's got it all worked out. Even the revolving-door legal setup of the Brooklyn Family Court. Why do you have to grow up so fast? Why do you have to know all this just because it happens to be true? And what am I supposed to do about it all?

"So I'm not talking to anybody," he says. And I see the line of Grandmother's jaw, miniaturized, when he stops talking. It's that little touch of inherited toughness, which I didn't inherit, that puts me over the edge. I pull back from him and start away. The tears that have been hanging around under my eyelids for weeks are back in full force, ready to let go. Always ready at the wrong time. "You going to school?" Byron asks.

"No," I say to the curtain, "I'm not going to the dumb-ass Van Cortlandt Academy today." I can feel his awed look through the back of my head. He thinks my school is Yale University, but classier. "I'm going down to the cafeteria for coffee. I'll be back in a while. You want me to bring you anything?"

"I guess not," he says in a thoughtful voice, psyching me out.

But I never make it to the cafeteria, where I wasn't heading anyway. I was planning on going down to the waiting room, which is full of Spanish-speaking people who know the value of tears and who cry if they want to, in unison and in groups. And there I'm going to let go among strangers. And I am going to cry my damn eyes out. Except I don't get there either.

A couple of steps from Byron's door I'm face to face with this tall, skeletal guy with a paunch and thin hair. I know him from somewhere, way back. And just as he asks, "Is this Brian Atwater's room?" I place him. This is the headmaster of Brooklyn Heights Collegiate. I remember him because I went to the lower school there a year when we first came to live at Grandmother's. And he hasn't changed. I have, of course, so I say, "I'm Jim Atwater, his brother."

"How is Brian?"

I let the wrong name pass once, not twice. "His name's Byron. Broken right clavicle. His arm's in a sling. He won't be writing any essays for the rest of this term."

This tells him I know he's from Byron's school. Still, he doesn't know me, so he says, "I'm Brewster Stewart, the headmaster."

We shake hands. "Can I see . . . Byron?"

"Sure. He'd like that." Then something makes me add, "Do you know Byron?" even though I have the answer to this one already nailed down.

"Well, I don't exactly know him," Headmaster

Stewart says. "I can't know them all, can I?" I let the answer to this one dangle. I ought to be glad he's bothered to come around, but somehow this doesn't cut much ice. "But maybe I could have a word with you first," he says.

I steer him away from the waiting room, and we find a couple of plastic chairs at the end of the hall. He plants enormous hands on his knees and clears his throat. You don't make Headmaster without public-speaking skills. "I understand that the boy—you boys—have recently lost your mother." He sidesteps the topic of our father. It's all there in the school records, which he's speed-read in preparation for this visit. "We were notified of Byron's accident by your grandmother, Mrs. Schermerhorn."

"Our grandmother is Mrs. Livingston. Mrs. Schermerhorn's a friend of Grandmother's. Makes calls for her, things like that."

Stewart absorbs this, probably getting a mental picture of Grandmother as senile and helpless. Ha.

• "And it was no accident. He was attacked by a gang whose methods sound reasonably professional. They beat him, robbed him, and then broke his collarbone. When you see him, you can imagine what kind of a fight he could put up. I think there were seven or eight of them, and they had wheels."

Stewart pulls thoughtfully on one long earlobe. "I see," he says. "Police called in?"

I think of Byron, then Grandmother, then the entire Kirby/Monday Evening Club power elite, complete with low-profile legal counsel. "Probably not."

Stewart gives this some thought. "And where did the . . . incident take place?"

"In the middle of Joralemon and Henry. He'd have had a better shot at crossing against the light in front of a truck."

"Ah, well," Stewart says, leaving his ear alone, "it was well away from school property then."

Even before I can work on the meaning of this—and the quetsion about the police—I'm beginning to tense up. Stewart's on his feet, ready to walk away. "I'll just stop in and say hello to Byron anyway. He has an excellent academic record, as I expect you know."

"I hope being mugged won't count against him, especially since it wasn't on school property."

This turns him around. "Was that an attempt at sarcasm?"

"To tell you the truth," I say, "I'm not sure. I can't quite figure why you're here except to make certain you're in the clear."

"I have a responsibility to all our students while they are within the school's jurisdiction. If you were older, you might be able to fathom the legal ramifications. As it is . . ." He gestures in the air, waving me out of existence. I decide not to go.

"Even without the jurisdiction and ramifications bit, though, it wouldn't look too good if word got around that Brooklyn Heights Collegiate kids are being creamed on the way home from

school. Might cost you a little credibility, and tu-
ition money."

"I can fully understand that you must be upset
about your brother's incident."

"Will you do me a favor and stop calling it an
incident? 'Incident' plays it down too much,
even for you." I'm beginning to roll now, even
with no history of getting mouthy with headmas-
ters. "If you feel any responsibility to your
kids—if you can feel anything—why don't *you* call
in the police?"

Stewart takes a deep, sighing breath, calls on
Heaven for patience in dealing with this malad-
justed, deeply troubled lad giving him a hard
time. "Surely calling in the police in an inci—
crime committed on a public street involving a
minor is the parents' responsibility."

"But we're running a little short on parents," I
fire back. "And as for my grandmother, Mrs. *Livingston . . .*" I let that go, let him remember his
impression of Grandmother as a drooling old vegetable.

"As you point out, I'm just a kid myself. It
looks like you're the logical one to call in the cops.
Who knows, this could be the start of a tremendous crime wave. They could be picking off your
students like flies. And as for the hospital taking
any action, you can forget that. They do well to
get the bedpans circulated—at a hundred bucks a
day."

Where I'm getting this line of argument from
I don't know. In a way I don't even want this
yo-yo in a vest calling in the police because Byron

doesn't want it. But I like seeing Stewart stew. It's making my day, and I haven't had what you'd call a good day in quite some time.

"Young man, what school do you go to?"

"What's that got to do with anything?"

"Just about everything. As you're not a student at Brooklyn Heights Collegiate, I'm under no obligation to you, legal or otherwise."

"For all you know, I *do* go to Collegiate. You wouldn't know your own students unless they fell behind in their goddam fees." I'm letting my voice get out of control, and it's echoing down the corridor, cutting down on the effect. But I'm through now, and Stewart's not going to walk away from me. I push past him. But before I get as far as Byron's door, I turn around. Stewart's still waiting for me to vanish. "And another thing," I say, loud and clear, "you can forget about that little visit to my brother's bedside. He can spot a phony every time."

I blunder right into the middle of a bunch of interns with clipboards, making the rounds with a real doctor. They step aside to make way for this crazy kid I am, manifesting early signs of hysteria, paranoia, whatever. And when they clear a little space around me, I see the tall, stooped figure of Mr. Carlisle Kirby stock-still behind them. I'm louder than his deafness. This is perfectly clear. He trains on me an old, watery, despairing eye. I lurch around him and head off down the hall, not knowing where I'm going. And no longer near tears. Tears? What do I need tears for?

"You feeding Nub?" Byron asks me that night. I forget where the day went. It's evening visiting hours. One dim shaded lamp next to Byron's pillow, and shadows. I've pulled the curtain back so he can see we have the hospital room to ourselves. We're alone all right. The Gray Panthers have decided to make themselves scarce as long as I'm keeping myself on an around-the-clock call. Mr. Kirby isn't going to be caught out in public with an unstable, yell-prone kid. Mrs. Schermerhorn has sent the usual bunch of red, white, and blue carnations. She's enclosed her calling card, engraved by Tiffany. No cutesy message of get-well-quick written on it. Cutesy messages are not her style, if she has one.

Am I feeding Nub? That is a tough question. I forget about Nub for long stretches because Nub's two greatest talents are keeping to himself and sleeping.

Byron says, "Nub eats a half can of Gourmet Feast in the morning and a soft pack of Tender Vittles at night. He snacks on Kat Krunchies, so I keep a bowl full for him."

"Ah . . . ," I say, "I'll look into it. Almah's probably feeding him." On the other hand, Almah's probably not feeding any ex-stray who sheds all over the carpets.

"If she's feeding him on table scraps"—Byron sighs—"he'll start throwing up in corners."

Almah has no table scraps, ever, as we both know.

"Well," Byron says with the calm that passes all understanding, "there's plenty Gourmet Feast and

Tender Vittles and Kat Krunchies. I always keep a good supply."

No direct request that I rush home and feed Nub. No whining, no wringing a promise out of me that I won't let old Nub starve. Nothing so easy. There's so much of Grandmother in this little kid that I feel outnumbered.

"I'll feed Nub." An even greater calm falls all over the hospital room. "I'll let him into your room so he can sleep on your bed if he wants to." I want to promise other, more fantastic things on Nub's behalf. Freshly caught mice, hand filleted, a rhinestone flea collar, an extra distemper shot for complete health coverage. I let it go with the original offer. And all this time Byron is thinking. I feel little sonar beams of intense thought radiating in this peeling green room. Byron's moved on from Nub. Like I say, he doesn't harp or whine. Also, he doesn't ask when he can go home from the hospital. After all, why should he be in any hurry to return to the outside world?

"Remember how we used to sit on the stairs Monday nights sometimes?"

This comes out of left field, of course. I'm not prepared, but I know what he's talking about. He means him and me and Mom, and how we used to creep halfway down the front stairs on Monday Evening Club night and listen to the oldsters conducting their session.

Mom wrapped up in her bathrobe with cream all over her face, and Byron and I edging very quietly down as far as the top of the parlor doorway, like three kids eavesdropping on the adults.

We had a whole routine worked out about avoiding the stairs that creaked and finding the right level where we sat in a row to hear Mr. Carlisle Kirby chairing the meeting: asking Mrs. Schermerhorn to read the minutes, calling on Mrs. Garrett Pierrepont to give the financial report, making a small joke about how Mrs. Dykstra is to maintain order because she's sergeant-at-arms. Most of the meeting's taken up with Sanka and Robert's Rules of Order.

I remember how Mom would fold her bathrobe under herself as we silently settled, and how our elbows touched as we sat there. Nudging each other, trying to crack each other up without letting ourselves succeed. I can remember Mom's presence between us, her hands clasped around her knees. She was tall, like Lorraine, but more graceful. I remember her hands, the length of her fingers, the tapering nails. But I don't try for any more personal details. After all, we were sitting there together in the dark.

Why is Byron remembering this? It's been months since Mom felt well enough to sit on the hard step in the drafty hall. "Sure I remember," I tell him.

"You think Grandmother knew we spied on her meetings?"

I'm sure she did. She probably even wanted us to carry on the good work of the Monday Evening Club in our own time.

"I can remember way back," Byron says, this old duffer recalling his youth. "But I couldn't figure out why they were always trying to do something for that one man, that Mr. Nixon."

This calls for an answer far more complicated than cat food. It's weird too because the subject of Mr. Nixon is practically the only topic Grandmother's ever discussed with me. And she only raised it once. "I don't know what they're telling you in school, if they're telling you anything," she said to me, "but it remains very fashionable to excoriate President Nixon. I trust you are aware of this, Jim."

I was—barely—and this was also the moment when I learned the word "excoriate," an excellent Grandmother-type word.

"He remains a favorite whipping boy for a nation that has lost a crucial war. The Vietnam War," she adds, leaving nothing to chance. Of course she's right. We learn nothing about it in school except that Nixon was a shifty liar who broke into hotel rooms and would bug your phone before he was caught and sent away to San Clemente, which may or may not be a foreign country.

Grandmother sees that this is not a hot issue with me. "I have no intention of compensating for all the distortions and omissions of your schooling, Jim. If I did, there wouldn't be time for anything else. Mr. Nixon ended the war, and whether that was a good thing or not remains to be seen. But it was a very bad thing for his enemies: the Pentagon, the arms manufacturers, the labor unions, the shipping magnates. A great many powerful people were profiting by the Vietnam

War. When President Nixon brought it to an end, his enemies took their revenge. He had far worse enemies in his own camp than in Peking or Hanoi."

I get a little delirious here because I'm rotten at geography. I'm not red-hot at history either, if that's what this is we're talking about.

"I have never tried to form your opinion upon any subject," Grandmother says in this long-ago session we have. "But there is something I want you to remember. I won't mention it again. President Nixon ended the draft—after more than thirty years of forced military conscription in this country. This means that unlike earlier generations of young men, you won't have to face two or more years of obligatory army life, or leave the country to avoid it. This gives you back two years that belong to you, and perhaps much more. You can pursue an education, a career, without interruption. President Nixon gave you your freedom."

I get a sudden flash of ex-President Nixon as a bronze statue in Borough Hall Park, freeing the slaves. I've never heard Grandmother on a soapbox before or after. Even at the Monday Evening Club session you never hear her voice except when she leads the Pledge of Allegiance. She's this mute, impressive presence in the wing chair who could take the floor any time she wants to, and so doesn't.

"Of course," she adds, "the draft will be re-instituted in the future. It's too lucrative for a great many faceless, nameless people who will gladly grow fat at the expense of young people's time and lives. And they will bring back the draft in some future Democratic administration. I can only hope you will be beyond the age of vulnerability. I hope they won't make you do their dirty work, Jim."

This is as tender as I ever remember Grandmother being, the way her look stayed on me for a moment. Then she turned on her cane, and that was all there was to it.

Byron is still waiting for a clear, sensible answer about Richard M. Nixon. "I think they figure that politics is so full of crooks that one particular one shouldn't be singled out." This is about as puny an answer as I have ever given anybody on anything.

"I don't know," Byron says, rubbing under his nose. "I don't think they'd send him birthday telegrams if they thought he was a crook."

How true, how true. But this isn't to be the major topic of the evening. Byron lets the whole subject drop. Scratch the Fiend of San Clemente and his faithful friends in the Monday Evening Club. And Byron's had the last word on the subject. Shades of Grandmother again.

What he's doing is leading me carefully back into the past. "What do you remember about way back?" he says. "About Dad?" This is the whammy we've been heading for through the Nixon smoke screen.

Okay, what do I remember about Dad? Not much. I was nine when he went, and less mature than Byron is at eight. I remember . . . what?

Things you can picture that don't translate out in words. Swinging on Dad's belt buckle for one thing. This goes back to the dawn of time. But I remember riding the flume at Six Flags outside St. Louis with him, wedged into this fake log with seats, shooting artificial rapids, hanging on for dear life, hanging onto him. I can remember cooking out at a campsite, sleeping out, with Lorraine and Mom and Dad and me in sleeping bags. I remember Christmases—stuff like that.

But I can't replay all this for Byron. Because they're all happy memories. And he doesn't remember any of them. And why should he have to wear my hand-me-down memories? They wouldn't fit.

So I lead him astray. "This is after Dad, but did I ever tell you about the time Lorraine saved me from the killer dog?" Byron looks at me. He never had much of a relationship with Lorraine either. She was too much older. Also, he's heard the dog story before.

"Tell it," he says, willing to humor me.

I jump into the story and try to remember how it goes because he'll remember details from before. "Well, I was about ten—eleven tops. Lorraine was in college. This is before she dropped out and got married." My sister Lorraine doesn't look like any of us. She's a big, towering, thick-legged girl. I always remember her in jeans and sweat shirts, a walking offense to Grandmother. In other ways, she and I are somewhat alike, emotions kind of close to the surface, with uncertain control.

"One night it was really hot," I tell Byron.

"And Lorraine and I walk over to Baskin-Robbins for ice cream. Anyway, we're coming back down Hicks Street when toward us comes this little old woman with a big dog pulling at the end of a chain-link lead. I'm not sure of the breed now—make it a Doberman. Definitely an attack dog. He gets up close to us and notices those ice-cream cones. He makes a lunge at me. I don't have time to get worried. Suddenly this big paw is splayed out across my chest, and all I see is this enormous slobbering mouth. The top dip on my cone hits the sidewalk. The big Doberman drops down right away and starts lapping it up. He has a tremendous taste for fudge ripple.

"This is no big thing. Even if the dog's rabid, we're practically home free while he licks all the way around the ice cream, not even coming back for the second dip. But there's this little old woman at the other end of the leash. She looks really worried for a minute. Then she yells out, 'Leave my dog alone! He never bothers strangers unless they bother him first!'

"I thought this was pretty astounding. I wouldn't have later on because I saw her around a lot, being dragged by that dog along every street in the Heights. And yelling at people who aren't even there.

"But this drives Lorraine crazy. She starts quivering like jelly and says to this old woman, 'Listen, you old fool, you better get that dog off the street. He attacked my brother, and I'm going to have the police in on this, and you'll be back in a padded cell before you know where you are!'

I've never heard so much hate in a human voice. Never.

"The old woman blinks like Lorraine is the insane one. She's used to people avoiding her, of course. 'Police?' she screams out. 'We'll see who has the police! That snot-nosed kid went for my dog! I seen him! Police! Help! Somebody get the police over here!'

"Of course nobody did. And the Doberman and I are just standing around waiting. And I'm still reasonably sure that Lorraine and the crazy woman are going to start mixing it up with fists and hatpins and whatever. The Doberman keeps lapping up my ice cream, making long tongue strokes on the pavement. And the woman goes on raving.

"Then Lorraine reaches down and seems to be going to rub the dog under the neck. But she unfastens the leash from his collar instead. Of course he just goes on eating my ice cream.

"And Lorraine swings her foot around sideways and connects with his rump, hard. The dog gives a startled jump and realizes he's free. So he lights out between two parked cars and sprints up Hicks Street. He's almost out of sight before the old woman sees she's holding a limp leash.

" 'Oh, my Gawd,' she whispers. 'Oh, my Gawd in heaven!' She darts out into the street—screaming, carrying on. It's really awful—begging her dog to come back, though he's already around the corner of the Bossert Hotel and probably traveling hard.

"He must have come back because I saw them

around later. But the way Lorraine acted shakes
me up at the time. What if he's gone for good?' I
say to her. 'The dog, I mean.'

"'Better for him if he is,' she says. 'If I see
him again, I'll kill him.'" This is old nonviolent,
sentimental Lorraine talking.

Byron listens to this retold tale with his usual
patience. In fact, more. He's staring off into space
past my shoulder. If he didn't look so alert, I'd
think I'd talked him into a trance. Besides, it's
not that good a story. For one thing, it's about
Lorraine and me, so it leaves Byron out. For another, there's a parallel here that strikes me in the
retelling. A parallel which I'm sure Byron grasps.
I felt smothered by all Lorraine's fierce protec-
tiveness. She was slopping over with love—there's
no other way to put it. And because of this she
was leaning on me hard. Maybe she felt Dad's
leaving worse because she was older and because
she was a girl. Maybe it was just this emotional
thing with her. I was glad when she got married
and left, though I never admitted it to myself.

And what if I'm doing the same thing to Byron—smothering him? I decide fast that there's no
parallel. I have to look out for him because he
doesn't actually have anybody else. And I don't
fight all his battles for him, do I? Otherwise, would
he be in this hospital bed?

Time passes while I'm dealing with myself
over this. But Byron's staring over my shoulder.
If he didn't blink once in a while, I'd be worried.

Visiting hours are about over. The warning

bell's rung. Footsteps in the corridor. Doors creaking. Byron blinks again. At last I turn around, follow his gaze. And I see there's somebody inside the door, standing there, maybe for some time. Enjoying this wonderful saga about Lorraine over-reacting to a dog. But this is somebody who hasn't heard the story before.

This is—it can't be, but it is—this is Dad standing there. In the same rumpled suit from the funeral, with a flight bag in his hand. Dad looking travel-worn, as if he'd been suddenly sent for, which he has.

Seven

The flight attendant—a gorgeous blonde in a snappy wrapper printed all over with the airline logo—gives Byron's slinged arm a look, then another at Nub in his cat carrier. Then back to Byron. I've buttoned a short-sleeved shirt of my own around him, with room inside for his angled elbow beneath the shirt sleeve that flaps pathetically. For days now he hasn't let me feed him. He's learned how to eat and perform other personal functions with his left hand. Of course the kid turns out to have latent ambidextrous tendencies.

"Listen, chief," she says, "I don't know how you got that animal all the way to the aircraft, but it's supposed to be checked with the baggage. No pets in the passenger compartments."

This is absolutely no complication. Byron already has one foot on the plane. I'm behind him, and behind me is a long line of Florida-bound pilgrims snaking all the way back to the boarding lounge. Maimed Byron just looks up at her with solemn, sensitive eyes, not even acting. "Oh, well," says Miss America of the Airways, "you keep—whatever it is—in its cage, okay?" She reaches out to pat Byron, but he's all elbow and eyes. So she grins him past her. Her head bobs a little—let's live dangerously on this flight. Rules are made to be broken.

Score one for Byron. Nub travels with us. Pets have been known to depressurize suddenly in the baggage hold anyway, and the blonde knows this. Besides, it's the arm in the sling that blows her away. There could be a large gray rat with rabies in the carrying case. Nub can't be bothered to push his whiskered face against the screenwire window. He's sitting in his miniature R.V. with his tail slapped against the opening.

We've gotten Nub past check-in and through the passenger shakedown for concealed weaponry, courtesy of Mr. Carlisle Kirby, who's seen us off. While he blustered at the checkpoint, Nub rode right through the X-ray machine like a piece of hand luggage, which he is. Being X-rayed to make sure he isn't a cat-shaped bomb will probably give him some fatal disease, but he's still with us.

We're already working down the aisle of the Florida plane, looking for our seat assignments. I let Byron carry Nub's case in his good hand. There are more attendants on this plane, which has three seats on each side of the aisle. All the window seats are taken up by big-gutted businessmen who won't even look at the view. Oh, Lord, if I am ever a middle-aged businessman, don't give me a fat gut. Make me jog. Make me steam. Make me work out till I drop.

So Byron won't even see out the window. We settle into aisle seats opposite each other, and Byron shoves Nub's case under the seat ahead of him. We're strapped down and ready for blast-off.

I have only myself to blame for this whole thing. In the countdown to summer, we were measuring in days. We could have moved from schools to camps without any trouble to anybody, especially ourselves. Even Byron's arm wasn't a major drawback.

No, I'm the well-known straw that breaks the camel's back because of my explosion at Byron's headmaster—badly timed and witnessed by Mr. Kirby. The Senior Citizen jungle telegraph lights up like a switchboard. Drums throb in the Brooklyn Heights wilderness. Word gets back to Grandmother, who's known all along that one or both of us will get out of hand one of these days. And I have. I've trodden lightly around Grandmother for many years, and I have blown it in one minute. Now that I've started rebelling against authority, it could develop into a habit. It's true. It could. It felt good.

And so my dad is summoned from Florida. He flies up and stays overnight at the Bossert Hotel. Grandmother doesn't run a rooming house for ex-sons-in-law.

Byron's injury is the excuse, but Grandmother has a private audience with Dad, and I know I'm the big topic. Dad goes back to Florida on a morning flight, still shying from any direct confrontation with Byron and me.

Later Grandmother calls me into the middle parlor to give me fair warning of what's coming off. She's in the wing chair, with her Lucite cane tucked beneath. The strain of having encounters with both Dad and me in the same week is telling on her. She looks old, tired, still grieving for Mom, and I feel responsible for every wrinkle. Believe it or not, I love this old bird. It's easy to love her—she doesn't expect it.

This is not a good scene for her. In all her dealings, she has to be in charge, so the burden's on her. I never open my mouth. I have already opened my mouth—thus, this scene.

"I reared your mother," she says, setting things up. "You may have concluded that I—resent her for . . . the way she died."

I haven't thought about it particularly, haven't had to. It's too obvious. In Grandmother's private universe you suffer anything. And you never cheat. Not even death.

"I would have resented her dying anyway. I was prepared to." Her lips come together in a line above that rock jaw. It's easier to talk even about this than to come to terms with my case.

"I reared my daughter—your mother—and gave her my best. When she came back home with you three children, I took her in. I don't believe in divorce, but I wouldn't have turned you away from my door. I am not as stiff-necked as you suppose." Here she gives me a look that's almost an invitation of some kind. But I don't risk a re-

sponse. She already has me between two bases with
the ball in her hand.

Besides, I'm thinking too hard, though not exactly along her lines: someday this old lady will
die too, the last of her breed, frozen in her pose.
And one of the few encounters I'll have left to
remember is this moment. I'll think back on this
even if it hurts.

"Your sister, Lorraine, was a trial to me," she's
saying.

How true, how true. Klutzy Lorraine who cried
over old TV movies. Aimless Lorraine who
studied Ed. Psych. and married a sergeant she
picked up at a lunch counter. I have a crazed
mental flash of big Lorraine sweeping up a small
sergeant in her arms and trying to carry him out
through the revolving door at Chock full o'Nuts.

"I could never see allowing a girl simply to follow her own inclinations. And Lorraine had so
few." Grandmother isn't even on the subject of
Lorraine for Lorraine's sake. She's using her to get
across the idea that she's already raised her own
child; she shouldn't be expected to raise another
whole flock—especially us. The gap's too wide
now. I see this. I almost want to nod.

"Of course you boys were an even greater problem to me, especially after your mother was ill and
I couldn't be sure how much strength and judgment she had left for dealing with you."

Strength and judgment. Prime Grandmother-
type words. A whole creed.

"I have tried to know what was best since . . .

in these past weeks." Grandmother stops. Her fingers fidget on the chair arms. Something crosses her face. "If only you were both *older*," she says, "just a few years *older*." I can really feel for her. That's all I want myself. It's eerie how close we are and how far apart.

"If I could give you years of my own, I would!" she says in a voice suddenly so strong that it makes the skin on the back of my neck prickle. Then her voice is quiet again. "I'm going to send you down to your father in Florida."

My pupils must be dilating. I didn't see this coming.

"I can't manage, and I don't take on responsibilities I cannot discharge. You can come back, of course, but not until the end of summer. Then, perhaps, I . . ." She starts to say something about herself, about how maybe she'll be further from Mom's death and closer to her own idea of "managing." She switches away from herself in time. "You and Byron have your schools, your friends here. . . ." She looks around in her mind for other things we have, finds nothing, and lets it go at that. "You both need a father. Whether or not you can develop a relationship with him is out of my hands. I don't know what your memories of him are. They will mean very little now. You will not be starting over. You will be starting fresh."

Not a word against Dad, nothing about his strength and judgment, if any. Grandmother's never been seen carrying a grudge. Dad was never her responsibility.

And so we're off to Florida, with no back talk. And Dad is about to become a father.

I don't let myself think about it. I don't even tell Kit Klein I'm not going to take the counseling job in Vermont. I can't believe this is happening. I'm vanishing without a trace into off-season Florida with one somewhat crippled-up brother, an unresponsive gray cat, return tickets, enough savings money to make us all independent, and a canvas bag full of shorts and Lacoste shirts.

Byron's good arm is clamped on the chair arm, and his head's out in the aisle. He seems to be counting the house. The flight attendants are whisking late arrivals into their seats and taking drink orders. Byron's bright as a button. This is a lot better than Camp Arrow Rock. I'd like to think he'd rather spend the summer with me instead of without, but this point hasn't come up. He doesn't seem worried about an entire summer with an unknown father with a lousy track record for reliability. And for this I'm glad because I'm worried as hell.

After a long delay, our number comes up on the runway, and we take off. This is a tremendous kick for Byron even though he can't see anything. He's playing pilot. He has the keen look of Snoopy trying to fly his doghouse.

Somewhere over New Jersey this girl comes up the aisle from behind us. I've already spotted her in the boarding lounge. She's easy to spot. She steps over Byron and settles into the middle seat beside him. His head pivots, and he gives me a penetrating look. His entire face is trying to tell me something. But I'm not too attentive because I can see the girl in profile over his head. She's almost a knockout, with auburn hair still electric from the brush. She's wearing some kind of sundress and has this great scattering of freckles all over her shoulder. She reaches down to put a small case under the seat, next to Nub, and the light catches that auburn hair. Naturally she's not sitting next to me because this is the kind of luck I'm cursed with.

Byron's still staring at me, and his mouth's making strange shapes. His eyebrows are meeting over his nose. What's the matter with this kid? If he wants to swap seats, he's got himself a deal. I look at the girl again. She looks like an ad for something forbidden. She's also about my age, though I am willing to be any age she likes.

Byron's eyes are darting in every direction. He can't lean very far into the aisle because of his seat belt, but he heaves over my way, points at something, and whispers, "Give it to me. Quick."

He's pointing to an old boarding pass somebody left behind in the seat pocket ahead of me. I see his own pass sticking out of his sling. Maybe he's making a collection. "You want this?"

"Yes," he hisses, "but keep quiet." What's he up to? His whole mood is total cloak-and-dagger. I hand the pass over. More mystery. He pulls his own boarding pass out of his sling, replaces it with the old one, and then gives the girl an almighty nudge. She's turned full-face now: a true knockout. Her eyes widen, and she listens some more. She seems to be taking the boarding pass, plants it prominently in the seat pocket in front of her. But Byron's talking on and on. She gets in a few words, but very few. What a line this kid must have.

A stewardess crosses my line of vision. When next seen, Byron's staring straight ahead, looking innocent and a little bored. But pretty soon he's whispering to the girl again. And she's hunching over, whispering back. I watch the perfectly straight part of her auburn hair, and I still don't understand any of this. When she sits up again, she gives Byron a look I've seen people give him before, people who think he may be a midget disguised as a kid.

He turns to me and says, "I have to go to the rest room."

"So go."

"I can't masage by myself," he says, waving his slinged arm. This much I can grasp. He wants me to retire to the rear of the plane for a powwow. We troop down the aisle, and he stops dead in front of two vacant rest rooms. "Bend over," he says, "I can't talk out loud." Then I get the story. "She doesn't have a ticket," he whispers, wetting my ear. "She's a *stowaway*."

"Can't be."

"Is."

I know it can't be. I saw her getting her seat assignment in a legal manner. Still, Byron's getting a tremendous kick out of this. I play along. "But how do you know?"

"She finally confessed. When I gave her my boarding pass. This may not solve everything," he says, shaking his head. "They may make a head count."

"Wait a minute," I say. "You thought this up—out before she . . . confessed."

"Sure. I watched when everybody came on. I'm pretty sure she wasn't with the rest of us. So she had to be locked back here in the *toilet*." He points at a rest-room door in case I've forgotten what a toilet is.

I concentrate on keeping a straight face. "How come you gave her your boarding pass? Why didn't you give her the old one?"

He tries to be patient. "In case they look close, I have a *ticket*. She *doesn't*. Besides, they saw me and Nub come on board."

I can be as sober as he is. "You know this is illegal, of course."

"She has to get to Florida," he explains.

"Is she a runaway?"

"I don't know," he says. "Maybe." The idea appeals to him. "Probably."

"How does she pull this scam?"

"She didn't want to tell me, but finally she did. She knows the airport like the palm of her hand." He holds out his palm. "She knows how to board just before the flight crew does. She's done it before. She didn't want to tell, but finally she did. One time they caught her, but they didn't do anything to her. She pretended she was epileptic."

We're both thinking this is a very inventive

girl, but not for the same reasons. I stare at him, not wanting to spoil this wonderful trip he's on all by himself. "You know," he says, "epileptic." His tongue lolls out, and his eyes roll around.

"Oh, good grief," I say. "Let's swap seats. I want to talk to her."

"I'm telling you exactly what she admitted," he says.

"There are other reasons for wanting to sit next to her."

We troop back up the aisle. Byron says over his shoulder, "Her name's Adele Parker." I hope after he's gone through puberty he still has his talents. He's had her eating out of his hand.

"You sure that might not be her code name?"

He shrugs, frowns, adds this to his profile of her. I ease into his old seat. Byron flops into mine and becomes instantly wrapped up in "Emergency Instructions for the Boeing 727." He's going to cover for us. "Well," I say, how's it going, Adele?" I figure Byron's broken the ice in his own unique way.

"A little strange so far," she says, slanting a look my way. "Is he really your brother?"

"Really."

"He's dynamite."

"He is that. His name's Byron."

"Byron?" Adele tilts her head. Her nose comes to a perfect point, history's most beautiful bird dog. "Byron's such an old-man's name."

"Therefore it fits him," I say.

"He's got an unbelievable imagination," she

says. She's not totally convinced of my own grasp on reality. "They had me back in the smoking section, which I can't stand, so I moved up. And just to keep the record straight . . ." She has an open-topped carryall in her lap. She parts the top with two fingers, and there's her plane ticket with the rim of her own boarding pass stuck in the folder. We both look at it in silence while Byron across the aisle is reading every word about the Boeing 727. He's whipped the system on behalf of a damsel in distress with larceny in her heart, and he is very pleased with himself.

"Listen," I murmur, "thanks for not putting him down. Did you actually tell him you have an epileptic act?"

Her tongue lolls out, and her eyes roll around. "Okay, okay." I glance over at Byron. He's caught this and nods with a quick I-told-you-so look. Strung up between the two of them, I'm somewhere between cracking up and wanting to make an all-out play for Adele Parker. Naturally, I don't do either. Something stirs, bumps, and hisses under my feet.

"What *is* that?" Adele draws up her feet; her eyes go wide again. They're green with gray flecks in them. Her eyebrows are almost invisible.

"Oh, that's our cat," I say, somewhat lamely.

"Speaking of stowaways." Adele looks heavenward. The attendants are racing up and down the aisle, bringing lunch. "Does he watch a lot of TV?" Adele asks.

"No," I say, "he just sleeps, sheds, and uses his litter box a lot."

"I mean *Byron*," she says.

My face is suddenly on fire. Why is it every time I'm around a girl, my I.Q. drops a quick fifty points?

"I mean he worked up an instant plot about me smuggling myself onto a plane in about two seconds. It sounds like TV."

"No." I struggle to say something that makes sense for a change. "He never watches. You see him in his natural state. He doesn't need TV."

Lunch comes. I plan to keep the conversational patter going. This is the time when discussions can die, while you're struggling to get the plastic fork ripped out of its cellophane sack. Besides, I have this need to change the general image Adele's getting. Spacy little brother, bumbling big brother, cat traveling economy—in short, a zoo.

But I notice that Byron's starting with his banana pudding, bypassing the chicken and green beans. "Leave the dessert till last," I tell him across the aisle.

"You really do the big-brother thing, don't you?" Adele says, starting on her salad, in case I start ordering her around.

"Not especially," I say, too quick. She's probably been bred not to call people liars. But I'm talking away like crazy now. Words flow out of me, even a late introduction. I tell her we're going to spend the summer with Dad. She's going to Miami to spend the summer with her mother. Her father in New York has custody of her, but her mother has these vacation-visit rights. I skip over

the fact that Mom's dead. Adele gets the idea that
our parents are divorced too. This is near enough
the truth; I'm not looking for sympathy. What
I'm looking for I don't try to picture. The airways seem filled with the children of broken
homes, migrating like birds.

She goes to Spence—a very statusy-type school—
my year, senior-to-be. I've never been elbow-to
elbow with a Spence girl before, even at a mixer.
She knows Kit Klein through a friend of hers who
lives in his building. I'm not sure whether she
knows him from his pre-couth, tough-shitsky days
or not, so we don't linger over this.

It comes out that I've never been to Florida
before. "What's it like?" I ask her.

She thinks. A tiny silver chain around her neck
nestles in the hollow of her throat. Beyond her,
past a fat businessman, the clouds stand still.
"Florida is sort of . . . mindless," she says finally.

This sounds good to me. I'm tired of thinking.
My brain turns damp and humid at the idea of
"developing a relationship" with Dad. I could get
worked up against the whole idea of it, except my
elbow is touching Adele Parker's. She asks what
Dad does for a living. I realize I don't know.
"Maybe nothing."

"There's a lot of that down there," she says.

I like the cool Spence-ness of her. Since we're
the same age, she's not playing a role, even though
she was born knowing how. She's over the Spence
hump: the moving in a pack, the passing of the

joint from some parent's private stock, the "sleep-ing over" at marathon slumber parties in some-body's penthouse on Park. And she's not pushing anything with the Radcliffe-Mount Holyoke-Ben-nington plans for after next year.

Her past flashes before me. She's grown up in Indian Trail shoes, an ocean of shampoo, an atom of makeup; her toenails have never known kinky color. She's never been near a Barbie doll. For the first ten Christmases of her life she was taken to Lincoln Center for *The Nutcracker*. She's never danced with another girl, not even in junior high. She studies without stereo. I wonder if she'd talked to me if we weren't strapped into adjoining seats, but this is the kind of thing I'm trying to stop wondering about. So I do.

Incredibly, we're touching down at Miami International. Too soon, too soon. We're taxiing now, looking for the gate, lumbering earthbound. Nub's probably standing up in his case, staring with amazement at the floor. The New York types are already on their feet, snapping shut attaché cases like castanets. "I'm going to make a run for it," Adele whispers. I try to get my legs out of her way, but the backs of her knees brush against me.

"I want to make it look good for Byron." She gives him a great, lady-spy look; then she's up the aisle, weaving past the businessmen, vanished in a disciplined cloud of bright hair. But I've man-aged to get her Miami address, and I've written it with an unsteady hand on the boarding pass.

Byron and I let the aisle clear before hustling Nub out. "We better not mention helping a stowaway to Dad," Byron says. "We better be careful what we say to a stranger."

Eight

He—Dad—is standing at the gate, at this our third meeting of the season. But this one has got to take. He's wearing a pair of white tennis shorts, a denim shirt with turned-back cuffs, white socks with blue bands, and Adidas sneakers. It could be worse: gold chains around the neck, flowered body shirt open to navel, polyester leisure suit, patent-leather loafers.

The airport is Someplace Else, exotic. Dusky Latin beauties trip along in heelless platforms, heading for flights to Ecuador, Nicaragua, Caracas, swinging Saks and Neiman-Marcus shopping bags, wearing oversize purple-lens shades. All rose-in-the-teeth types. The p.a. announcements are in Spanish and English. We are off our turf.

It's high noon, or at least it feels like it. The sun falls in vertical lines, even indoors. We shake hands with Dad. Byron's sober as a judge. "Judge" may be the word. Dad gives Nub a slight double take. But then what's one more—or less?

We drive out of the airport tangle past the first palm trees shaking in the flight patterns. WELCOME TO MIAMI AMERICA'S FUN-IN-THE-SUN PLAYGROUND, followed by another billboard, splashier: BURIAL FOR TWO ONLY $295 COMPLETE. Dad has maybe the first Datsun ever introduced into this country. Bright orange, Simonized over banged-up bodywork. It isn't air-conditioned. You could bake brownies on the seat.

We thread through narrow streets, past little white cottages with electric-blue trim and religious grottos in swept yards. Very foreign. Tidy but temporary. Then we're on a sort of country road angling through the city. Enormous trees—banyans, Dad says—a dozen trunks snaked around each other and big umbrellas of foliage above, dappling the road. A bike path runs parallel, with cyclists wearing only sweatbands and shorts, pumping along beside us.

We pass a sign, COCONUT GROVE BUSINESS DISTRICT, and follow the arrow. Who is he? Lush? Lecher? Playboy? Pauper? All the above? The bonding on the Datsun's windshield is loose, breaking down the light into its component, rainbow parts. It hits Dad's legs. Tennis player? Swimmer? Over-the-hill jock? Who knows? Wait and see. Plenty of time. An entire summer in a place with no other season.

We swing off the road, through the gate of a wall holding back jungle. Wind in through a track behind a big, balconied, raw-new apartment building, chalk-white above the green. The road wanders, years older than the building, through the bottom of an aquarium. Behind the high rise, hidden away, a damp little bungalow squats in sand and high grass. Practically an Aztec ruin compared to the new high rise. Porous coral stone walls, fading pink under a low tile roof. "This is it," Dad says, pulling into what yard there is. A solitary vine grows up over the entire house. I hear Byron thinking: is there room for all of us here? I wonder myself. It looks like a single unit cast adrift from a motel.

Dad cuts the engine. "The high rise is a condominium—the Barnacle Cove. I manage it. The house comes with the job."

Okay, we know a little bit more now. He's got a job, whatever it is. Janitor? Agent? Doorman? Window washer? What does a manager manage? I manage to get out of the car. My shirt peels away from the vinyl seat.

Dad reaches for Nub's case, but Byron has shifted it around to his good hand. "I can do it," Byron says. Good for you, kid. Show him. Show him what?

There are two bedrooms—cells side by side, and Byron and I get them. Dad's going to sleep on a couch in the living room, which is also a kitchen, divided by a counter. It's all musty but orderly. Clean clothes from a laundromat on the counter top, white socks folded in on themselves, army style. Byron and I get our room assignments. The situation's weird and familiar somehow, like the first day of the first year at camp. A summer of strangeness without idea number one about how to deal with it.

Byron has a small case for his clothes. I see Dad unzip the top and hand it to him in a single gesture. He knows one-handed Byron would labor over that zipper. But Dad doesn't try to do more. A nice touch, I have to admit.

I hang around in my eight-by-eight room as long as I can. There isn't that much to unpack. I commit the room to memory, wishing it was a memory: single bed, chest of drawers, tile floor brittle but not gritty, Venetian blinds but no curtains. There's something very boot camp about this barracks, but I have no complaints coming. I should kiss the walls because I have it to myself.

I'm standing around in this room that looks swept clean of clues. But clues to what I don't know. And I'm thinking hard now. When I open the door between me and Dad, it's confrontation time. I don't know how it's going to go or how it's going to affect Byron. But we're just one warped plywood door away from a general clearing of the air. We are going to lay some ground rules.

I get around to opening the door. Nub's out of his case and deeply asleep on the refrigerator top, spindly haunches drawn up in a hump. He's shaped like a 1939 Plymouth. Dad's shucked off his shirt and has on a pair of faded red trunks. "I thought we'd have a swim."

So much for the big scene. I go back in my room, pull open the drawer where I think I've stashed my trunks. There's a totally different

swimsuit in this drawer, female style: a bikini bra
for some unknown, trim little figure. Bright flowers on a black backbround make an expressive
little two ounces of nothingness. A clue unswept
away. Or maybe not. Maybe this particular item
is left here because nobody's erased any clues.
Maybe we're all open and up-front here. Or would
be if anybody could say anything. I open the
right drawer and find my trunks and pull them on.

The pool belongs to the high rise, at the far end
of a path of crushed white shells. All around are
bulldozer scars where they've carved all this instant luxury out of a swamp. Nobody's at the pool.
The Barnacle Cove's inhabitants, if any, are sealed
behind brown-toned windows in their air-condi-
tioning.

There's a kiddies' wading pool across the patio,
with a very tame slide slanting into it. Byron
walks past it without a look.

I'm ready to dive in from the side of the big
pool when I remember Byron can't go in the
water with that sling, much less swim. Dad, of
course, hasn't given this a thought. He's probably
one of those everybody-in-the-pool types. He's
busy making a pile of towels, a shirt and pants of
his own, and a beeper—those things doctors wear
on their belts that signal them to call the hospital.
Except he's no doctor. I see he's letting Byron
find his own way to the far end of the pool. It's
practically Olympic size, though kidney-shaped,
this being Florida. Wide steps go right down to
the bottom at the shallow end. Byron steps out of
his thongs, hops once on the frying concrete, and

walks down the steps into the water. He moves experimentally. The green water climbs up his white body to within inches of his arm. He back-steps and sits down on the steps in the water with the sling just grazing the surface. He looks around at the water with little eyes slitted against the glare. A jet-black beach ball floats toward him. He bounces it out of the pool with one foot. He s improvising a game that will keep the ball in play within range of his foot. One of his moods of complete calm is settling over him.

I dive from the side into the deep end and fight down until I can slap my hand on the bottom. The water's too warm at the top, but below it's like a night in the mountains. I think seriously about living the entire summer underwater, without benefit of scuba.

When I surface, Dad's sitting on the edge half-way down the pool, with his legs in the water. We're not going to be treated to any trick dives off the high board. I swim myself into a half-daze. Incredibly, the sun's actually beginning to shift off dead center. It must be five o'clock. Maybe not. Maybe only four. Dammit, at this rate we'll all be old men before this summer's over.

Finally I pull up out of the water a calculated distance from Dad. His beeper starts sending out a signal. He gets up, grabs a towel to dry his legs, and pulls on his clothes. "Probably somebody to look at an apartment," he says, nodding toward the building. "Want to come along?"

I shake my head, and he starts off, jamming his feet into his tennis shoes as he goes. At the end of

the pool, Byron has the beach-ball game down to a
science, almost juggling it out of the water with
his feet. He's getting the maximum mileage out of
this pool without even getting half wet. He's settling in.

"You want to eat in or out?" It's actually evening, practically, and we're all back from the pool
and showered. Nub's been taken out once to do his
business in the sand outside the door. The biggest
litter box he's ever seen. He's scratched around and
dampened Florida in twelve separate places and
stared yellow-eyed up into trees full of invisible
rustling birds.

"I don't care," I say. It sounds sullen, but I
can't help that. I don't care whether we eat in or
out or if.

"Out then," Dad says. "I'll have plenty of time
to treat you to my cooking. You don't cook?"

Somehow in a room this small I can't look him
in the eye, even when I'd like to be staring him
down. "I'll try."

"No, it's okay," he says. "We'll manage."

I wonder.

We walk out into the evening and around the
Datsun. We're going on foot. It turns out that the
jungle plot Dad lives in is set down in a small
town, Coconut Grove, which is somehow ma-
rooned in Miami. And no place exactly relates
to any place else. Furthermore, Coconut Grove is
not your basic small town. Though it's half shut
down in the summer, it's a fairly funky place.
Beads, beards, beach bums, the Hamptons or

Greenwich Village ten years behind. They're still into macrame.

We stroll past a somewhat chi-chi place called the Coco Plum, jammed with people eating crepes in white iron chairs. I learn later that there are only two other bona fide places to eat in the Grove. Lum's, a routine short-order spot disguised behind driftwood siding, and a place with no name. We go into the no-name place, which is not trying to be anything but a diner with mimeographed menus. It's not doing a great business.

We settle into a booth, and a waitress who's having to handle the counter and the booths comes over. "Hey, Howard," she says. I don't see the look he gives her because this place also turns out to be too small for looking Dad in the eye.

"Hi, Marietta," he says. "These are the boys." Not exactly an introduction. Evidently none needed. We're easing into something very casually. This Marietta seems to be in the picture already. I throw caution to the winds and give her a look.

Her eyes would be too big except they're violet blue with real lashes. The rest of her face curves in sharply from strong cheekbones that balance the eyes. I should be a painter and go into portrait work. Her face is heart-shaped, and her hair is like a black cap, twirled just a little at the ends. She's maybe twenty-four, twenty-five. I get that bell-ringing sensation that Interesting Older Women give me. Distant bells.

Even in her first three syllables there's a kind of Dolly Parton drawl in her voice, soothing-southern. She's not wearing an emblem T-shirt or a waitress uniform, just a middle-of-the-road white blouse over an old-fashioned apron banded around her only-big-as-a-minute waist. She's too thin, except it works. Her stock rises even higher on my private board when she gives Byron a fringed look without ruffling his hair or asking about the sling. Maybe she knows about the sling.

"What's for supper?" Dad says.

"These boys ever had grits up Nawth?" Marietta asks. I can feel her look fall on me, but I'm fooling with the salt and peppers.

"That's breakfast, Marietta," Dad says.

"Breakfast all day," she says, "our motto. You come back in the morning, sport. For grits." She taps my elbow with one finger. Being called sport is not my favorite thing, but she can make anything sound good.

There's more conversation. I think Dad must be starved for it. He banters back and forth with Marietta, all very familiar. So he comes here to eat a lot. So would I. She leaves without ever getting around to taking our orders. And comes back with an entire church supper. A Corning Ware dish of baked beans, ham-and-cheese sandwiches piled on a plate, French fries in a basket, coleslaw, pea salad, bright red Jell-O. Byron watches all the food covering up the entire table. This is not Almah's style.

"You cleaning out the refrigerator, Marietta?" Dad says.

"Bawd of Health," she answers, mysteriously.

Byron checks with me to see where to begin

this orgy. I'm lost. There must be a balanced diet in here somewhere if we can find it. The red Jell-O comes in parfait glasses. "Is this dessert?" he asks, giving me owl eyes and pointing straight down at it.

"There's three slabs of raisin pie set back," Marietta tells him, though I think she's looking at Dad. "That'll be dessert so save room for it, you hear?" She tucks a paper napkin into the neck of his shirt and goes back to the counter. I half expect her to slide into the booth with us.

"Home cooking," Dad says, and starts passing dishes.

Marietta reappears when we've picked the table nearly clean. "What's the matter with my baked beans?" she wonders aloud. "There's a dab left." We rub our stomachs, roll our eyes, show appreciation with body language. "Well, I guess I'll have to tote it home in a paper sack," says this gaunt, gorgeous girl, mother-henning us. "Save your forks for the pie."

Byron looks at his fork in disbelief. We've never eaten this well out of Almah's kitchen, but there's always been a separate fork for dessert. But we're far from Almah. We are, as I say, off our turf.

I'm lying awake in a strange bed, thinking I haven't been asleep, though I have. No air conditioner in the only window, but the muggy dampness from the jungle outside passes for coolness. The trees are loud with country sounds. Subtropical birds complain bitterly. Insects sing grand opera. All kinds of rhythms going in the undergrowth. These are sending me to sleep and then bringing me back. I haven't counted on the night being twice as long as the day.

Then I hear inside sounds breaking away from the din outside. A little muttering of talk, high and low. A shuffle of feet somewhere not immediately outside my door. Water running. The house is alive, and suddenly I know we're all three awake, but I'm the only one alone. I can hear Dad's voice rumbling and Byron's answering.

I'm out of bed like a flash, grabbing around in the dark for my jockey shorts. The tile adheres to my feet. I crack the door, but the living room's dark. There's light past the refrigerator, outlining Nub's head and cocked ears up near the ceiling. The bathroom's just beyond the refrigerator.

I walk toward it. Byron's sitting on the edge of the bathtub. Dad's sitting beside him in a T-shirt and pajama pants. He's got his arm around Byron, whose breath is catching in his throat like he's in pain. He's rocking back and forth on the tub.

"What's wrong?" I say to him, stepping out of the dark.

"Nothing," Byron says, looking up quick, clenching the little knobs of his knees together. He's wearing only shorts, and his skin's already a little pinkish from the sun.

"His collarbone's hurting him," Dad says.

Oh, great, just when we get to the end of the world. "Is it bad?" I say to Byron, wanting to move in closer, except Dad's already there.

"Naw," Byron says, still rocking.

"I gave him aspirin," Dad says. "It'll take effect in a little while." I wonder how long they've been sitting there. "I heard him walking around in his room. It's going to be all right." He says this last part to Byron, and his arm's still around the slinged shoulder, lighting cradling it.

Feeling useless, I say, "I wonder why it's flaring up now."

"It always aches at night," Byron says. "It's like a bad headache, only it's here." He dips his chin down to his right shoulder. "It'll get better," he says, encouraging me. "But the doctor said I'll probably always be able to tell when it's going to rain."

This interesting item gets past me. "You mean you've been hurting before and didn't tell me?"

I'm suddenly back in Brooklyn Heights, going over nights past and beyond recall. And I see myself crapped out in my bed at the back of the house and Byron sitting on the edge of his bed at the far end of the hall, rocking back and forth because his splintered collarbone is giving him fits. He doesn't want to wake me up. And I have not given him one thought.

Then I practically go crazy. Dad's sheet-plastic bathroom walls wobble and flicker.

"Get away from him," I say, starting quiet. "I'll take care of him." Then the footgates really open up in my head. I'm cutting loose, louder and louder. "Damn you, get away from him!"

Dad isn't looking at me, but he isn't moving.

"Don't, Jim." Byron's shaking his head. "Don't say bad things."

But I'm chock-full of bad things, eight years' worth. "You! I'm talking to you!" Dad knows who I'm talking to. I'm leveling at him over Byron's head. "You leave him alone. You gave up your rights to him. You walked out before you ever heard his voice. You think you can make that up now with a couple of stinking aspirin? God damn you!"

Byron's whimpering now, ducking his head, running his fist across his eyes. But the tears are falling anyway. And Dad's arm stays around him, shielding him. And still I'm not through with all I've got to say. I haven't even gotten a good start.

Nine

I wake up in the morning, already remembering I'm at a tremendous disadvantage.

Nothing I've said—yelled—the night before has provoked my dad to deck me. So I've got something coming. He just let me run down, then walked past me like an old man. Not my old man. Just any old man. And I was left with Byron, who was finally coming apart. But these aren't the healing tears I've been waiting for from him since Mom died. I did this to him. I've pulled the rug out from under Byron.

Even getting out of bed takes a giant act of will. I have no idea what time it is. I've already stuffed my Seiko in a drawer. In a summer this long I've decided not to divide time artificially. This is not slated to be a season when you need a sweep hand. I get dressed and notice my hand reaching for the doorknob. I figure Byron's sleeping it off. I hope Dad's out of the house.

He's sitting at the counter in front of an empty cup.

"Why don't you go on up to Marietta's for breakfast," he says. I miss hearing that this isn't a question.

"I'll get something here." Though I don't have a leg to stand on, I'm walking toward the refrigerator.

"No," he says, "I'd just as soon you get out of the house for a while. I don't feel like facing you this morning."

I know the feeling. It's mutual. So I walk out into the morning, up toward the street. Coconut Grove is a late riser. A few cars out, fewer pedestrians. A panhandler type wrapped in a winter overcoat is just stirring on a park bench—Skid Row with palm trees. The bum has a great tan.

I drift around the streets, past the Dade cycle Shop and the Blue Water Marine Supplies. Up and down past little shops behind fake Spanish arcades. A bookshop, the Grove Book Worm, is doing some early business. "We Have *The New York Times*," says a sign in the window, enough to trigger twenty-four hours of pent-up homesickness.

Lum's is advertising a ninety-nine-cent breakfast, and I'm tempted by a completely anonymous place. But I'm heading for Marietta's and my feet know the way.

"Hey, Jim," she calls out before I'm in the door. She's got four or five at the counter and a boothful. Her grits rush hour. I start for the counter, then veer off to a booth. I'm settled into it before I remember she's been introduced to me, but I haven't been introduced to her. Funny how she can pull my name out of a hat, so to speak.

I'm scowling at the breakfast menu, which is smudged beyond belief and plastic coated. She comes up with a coffeepot, slips the menu out of my hand and replaces it behind the sugar bowl. "Gonna be hotter than a scalded dog today if it keeps up," she says.

I manage to glance up at her, at least as far as her blouse. Her breasts are small and apple-firm. "Get a smile out of you?" Her hand's on her hip, and I can see she's waiting me out. I work up a smile that feels cracked in three places.

"Well, for Pete's sake," she says. "I wisht I hadn't asked." She's gone then, but I know her routine. The menu's a mere formality. The coffee, while good, is a big mistake. It's clearing my mind. I'm thinking at the top of my lungs.

Marietta's back, scooting a platter in front of me. "We fry in butter," she says. "It makes that little difference." Why is it everything this straightforward girl-woman says sounds vaguely mysterious? It can't be the accent alone, which isn't that thick unless she wants it to be.

At one end of the platter we have a slice of ham, four strips of bacon, and numerous sausage links. At the other, scrambled eggs in a pile. Between is a vast mass of gray-white granular stuff. Grits. I eye them a moment too long.

"You salt 'em and you butter 'em," Marietta

says. "Orange, grapefruit, or for the desperate, prune."

"Excuse me?"

"What kind of juice you like? I know Yankees don't have grits, but you mean to tell me you-all don't have juice?"

"Orange, please. Marietta."

She's off toward the kitchen then, and I think she's humming, "Come to the Florida orange juice tree. . . ." She's as corny as *Hee Haw*, and I'd like to rest a hand on her breast. And she's going to cheer me up if it kills us both. I'm wondering why I can't play my role in this. Then I remember I have my reasons.

I start stuffed and then eat with a growing appetite on both sides of the grits. Then, giving in, I slide the fork into the grits, which I've salted and buttered up a storm. They aren't bad. I don't want any more. But they aren't bad.

Somewhere from a distance I have the sensation that someone is checking on my grits-eating.

She comes back as I'm contemplating the naked, steak-size platter. And she slides into the booth. "Hey, Marietta!" comes a voice from the counter. "How about some more coffee?"

"Just go around back there and hep yourself," she calls over, "and add it to your bill." This causes general merriment.

"Well, how you like Florida?" she says, smoothing out an invisible place mat before her. I look at her hands, her fingers thin between the joints. No rings? No ties? I think again of executing great paintings.

"You tell me," I say. "I'm a stranger here."

"It's heaven," she says, waving one of those hands around the totally tacky diner. She means it. "Where I come from, Florida is where you go when you die if you been good. I came on down early." For some reason I'm just barely following her train of thought.

"Listen"—she taps the table with one finger—"you come from Dothan, Alabama, and anything south of five miles north of Mobile looks like heaven on this earth to you. I remember the first time I saw the Gulf—around Panama City, Pensacola—Red-Neck Riviera, they call it—I thought: one day I'm going to keep a-going south until there is no more. And here I am. Miami's about as far south as you can go. Except for the Keys, and they've about got them ruint with them dope runners and what-all. Key West is a mess with all those weirdos from—"

"Up north?" I offer.

"All over," Marietta says, ladylike. I decide I have a natural affinity for people who don't look you in the eye. Her thumbnail traces invisible curving patterns on the table top, and her eyes follow, maybe seeing the patterns. I'm looking her in the lashes. Yet I know she's been studying me. And I like it, whatever her reasons are, even if she's seeing Dad in me.

"You'll see," she says. "You'll take to it down here. And your little brother will too. They got the Seaquarium and Planet Ocean and the Parrot Jungle and the Venetian Pool and dog races at Flagler. A snake farm, too, if that's your idea of a good time, and jai alai and the Goodyear blimp. I don't know anything about New York City, but oh, Lord, they got everything here a person could want."

"And what happens after a person's made the rounds of all the sights?"

"Oh well shoot, that'd take you a month of Sundays. I left out Walt Disney World up at Orlando, and Palm Beach, where Mrs. Got-Rocks lives, and—"

This is not the last time I hear of Mrs. Got-Rocks from Marietta. Mrs. Got-Rocks is her own private myth—the lady born with silver spoons sticking out all over her, who lolls around all day in Marietta's shifting idea of luxury: in a mirror-chrome bed dividing a mango with a solid-gold knife, wrapped in endangered species for a night at the opera, which is an art form Marietta takes on faith. To Marietta the world's an endless round of novelties, and she takes an innocent pleasure in the doings of the rich, forming and reforming them to fit into little pigeon holes in her mind. She's the most naïve person I've ever met, and full of wisdom. ". . . But of course it's the people who make a place," she's telling me, and her eyes want me to believe it.

"And what kind of people live in Miami?"

"Oh—people getting away, starting over. . . ."

"Hiding out?"

"Them too."

As far as I'm concerned, the conversation's skating near Dad. I'd like to ask her point-black if she's having a thing with him. The need to know leaves as fast as it came. I'd settle for a return to Mrs. Got-Rocks, but Marietta says, "Where's your daddy this morning?" spoiling everything.

"Sitting home in front of a coffee cup."

"He's a bear with hangnails in the morning," she says. "Like you."

"I don't know much about him. And I'm not too interested in being like him."

She gives me a look, runs a sweeping hand over the table top. "That's right," she says. "Be yourself. It's the best policy." She's pitched this bold pronouncement of mine back in my lap. I figure I've made her mad, since she gets up and walks away. But she's back with my check, hands it over with a perky flourish. It totals out at seventy-five cents. "Are you kidding, Marietta? This is ridiculous!"

"Got to undersell Lum's," she says, giving me a shrewd look, deadpan, mock-serious.

"At these prices you won't last the week," I tell her, meaning it.

"At these prices everybody in Miama should be eating here by the end of the week."

"Do you own this place, Marietta?"

"Shoot, no. If I did, I'd sell it. See you, sport." She drifts back to the counter, and I watch her go, the apron bow in the small of her back, the stockings glossing her slender legs above the bloblike waitress shoes. And I know she knows I'm watching her. She's been watched before.

I take my time heading back to the house. But he's sitting where I left him. He may not have moved. Not noticing the milky cornflakes bowl and the drained juice glass, I figure Byron's still asleep.

I guess Dad's dressed for work. His beeper's on his belt. He's wearing a spotless, unironed golf shirt. His face still has an early-morning look, what I see of it. I don't want to study that face too closely. I might see somebody I know in it. "Let's get it going," he says.

I decide to stand. Is it an item of interest to either of us that I'm taller than he is, marginally? "If you want an apology for last night—" I begin.

"I don't," he cuts in. "Apologies work between friends, occasionally between sons and fathers— nothing that covers our situation."

He's taking a fairly aggressive line, I see. I still have unspent ammunition from the night before, but the old steam just isn't there. To weasel out, I nod my head toward Byron's door, using this as an excuse not to talk. Or to be talked into anything.

"He's up and out," Dad says. "He wanted to go back to the pool."

Naturally, I picture Byron fallen into the deep end and floating there dead and bloated, sling out of the water like a broken mast.

"He'll be all right," Dad's saying. "If you give it some thought, you'd rather see him on his own than with me."

If I keep quiet, it means I'm giving this some thought, but I can't think of anything to say.

"He's out of earshot now, and if you want to

pick up where you left off and light into me, go ahead. If that's your seventeen-year-old idea of clearing the air, cut loose."

He places five fingertips against five fingertips and stares into the cage this makes of his hands. He's waiting. "That's too easy," I say.

"Meaning?"

"Meaning if I mouth off for ten minutes, that wipes your slate clean for eight years. Screw that." I jam my hands in my hip pockets and give him my back.

"Great," he says. "Then maybe we can talk some sense." He actually clears his throat, which seems to declare the negotiations open. In order not to be drawn in backwards, I turn around.

"You're raising your little brother, right?"

"Who else is going to do it?"

"Okay. I've dealt myself out a long time ago, and your mother—"

"Hold it right there." I jab a finger at him, try to make him look down the barrel of it. "Leave her out of this. Completely. I don't want to hear one word about Mom from you now or ever." I see it, or I think I do. He's comparing his cutting out on us with her doing the same thing. I'm not taking this from him, even to use it against him.

"A rule," he says. "I can abide by that. You're raising Byron, but you're under my roof. This is one thing we can't blame each other for. It doesn't take much imagination to see this was your grandmother's idea. If I'd made a claim on you both, she'd have thrown me out of her house. But once it was her idea to send you two down here, then it was fine. All I want to know is, where do we go from here?"

"How about back to the airport?" I say. I have his forehead in my sights. With a bit more effort, I could be looking him in the eye.

"Your grandmother's gone to a hotel in the Poconos for the summer with that friend of hers from Joralemon Street."

Typical of Grandmother not to tell me her own plans. Typical of me not to ask.

"I doubt if she'd put up with the idea of you two rattling around alone in her house all summer."

How true. And what a great idea.

"So we're stuck with each other," he says, "and I want some kind of idea how we're going to make it to Labor Day. If you don't tell me, then the ball's in my court, which I assume is the last thing you want.

"To take an recent example, when Byron—or you—gets sick in the night, I want to know whether to get up and look after you or pretend to sleep through it. As you'll be quick to point out, I've got no history of dealing with kids your ages. So you tell me, and I'll see if I can live with it."

The question's academic. After the stink I've caused, Byron wouldn't dare let his pain show again.

This guy, Dad, should have been a lawyer. He's talked me into a corner, and it doesn't even have that prepared-speech sound. If we've got any common ground, it's the impossible dream of getting through this summer in three pieces. To shut him up, I try to build on that. "I think we can make it," I say. Actually I mumble it, but he hears. "I don't have any master plan. Let's take it easy and . . . do what comes naturally. Let's call it a truce."

There are holes in this, but he ought to be satisfied with it.

"I don't know what truce means," he says, "but fine." He holds up his hand, one stubby finger in the air. "Byron's the unknown quantity in this, though."

"Not to me he isn't."

"At his age they change fast. Every day. In a lot of ways this summer's going to be longer for him than for us. At my age three months is nothing—even these. At your age—well, skip that."

"Better not," I say. "What's three months at my age?"

"You want to be nothing because you'd like to think you're already grown up."

"And how do you work that out?"

He raises his eyebrows slightly. "Because I was seventeen once."

I want to say: and you're probably still seventeen behind that sagging exterior. But I let it pass, wanting to get back to Byron, which he does.

"But he's going to be doing some growing up this summer. He's not going to be the same at the end of it, and in a few ways that have nothing to do with you or me."

I don't see what he's getting at. Later, I see,

but not then. "Don't worry about Byron. He's very mature for his age."

"No, he's not, as a matter of fact," says Dad, the big authority, the self-anointed Dr. Spock. "He's a typical kid, a little quiet, a little bewildered by the death . . . by a death in the family. And he's not a minute ahead of himself."

I ooze with sarcasm: "Of course you'd know with your vast experience of him."

"Could it be I can see him better than you can because I'm not breathing down his neck?"

"No."

"Okay. So that makes two people we're not going to be able to talk about. My ex-wife and your gifted brother. And as far as I'm concerned, you can add your grandmother to that list. It looks like it's just you and me, by your own decree. Anything else to cover before the truce?"

"Yeah, a couple of things." One of them's my karate chop, and I find I've had it ready all along. But it'll keep a minute longer; I save it for last. "Let's not have any talk about the so-called good old days."

"Which particular good old days?"

"I'm not surprised you've forgotten," I say. "I'm talking about the time before you walked out on us when Byron was four months old."

He eyes me. Runs his tongue around his lower lip. "Well, I suppose from your viewpoint that's going pretty far back in history to build anything on."

"I'm not interested in building anything. And let's not have any talk about the future either. No point getting Byron geared up about something he's not going to have. You might as well know one thing right now. After this summer's over, I'm going to see to it that he forgets we were ever down here."

Some of this speech comes to me as I say it. Dad sits there. He seems to listen even after I've run down.

"All right. More rules," he says. "Looks like we're stuck with the present. Remember, you called the shot. Anything else?"

"Yeah." Here it comes, the grand finale. "You sleeping with Marietta?"

He doesn't bat an eye. Here's his second opportunity to give me a fat lip—come on, creep, let me have it. He just lets the question hang for a long moment. "You're going to be easier than I thought," he says, "You've got no subtlety. Now."

He drops his fist on the counter top like a gavel. "The truce begins."

Ten

It's July somehow, and for maximum mobility and to work off steam Byron and I rent bikes from a place with a poem in the window:

> Buy a car nevermore
> Remember: Ten on the sprocket
> Not four on the floor

Byron's out of his sling, checked over by a local doctor looking strangely like a surfer: striped tank top under his white medical coat, a Moped in his reserved parking space.

We've pinked, peeled, and are working up authentic tans. Biking browns the shoulders, clears the head, or so I think before I come unstuck. We range all over the Grove and the territory across the Dixie Highway. And this is where I'm nearly totaled one innocent-seeming afternoon by

120

something that creeps up behind me. Not traffic, something else.

Byron's pumping along ahead of me, and I'm letting him outdistance me when we ride past a kind of vacant-lot park. There's a woman in the middle of the park, braving the heat and feeding two little kids a picnic on a couple of beach towels.

The light flickers through the palms, and I catch a glimpse of the woman in profile, do a double take, and nearly end up under my bike. My foot grazes the spokes. Even the little kids are familiar. One's staggering around on the towels; the other one's older, sitting still.

I squeeze the hand brakes, give the front-wheel brake extra grip. The rear wheel leaves the ground, and I nearly lunge forward over the handlebars. I've got to stop and make contact with these people. The bike wheels scrape the curb, and Byron's a half block ahead of me.

I plant a foot on the curb. The woman's not really close. But still I know her. She's coaxing the smaller kid to eat something, and I know the gesture of her out-stretched hand and the way she balances back on her arm. I know that coaxing little movement, and I can almost hear her familiar voice.

I ease the bike flat, forget about Byron, who hasn't looked back. I'm across to the sidewalk and then a step or two into the park. The smaller kid sits down suddenly. His legs fly up. I hear the woman's familiar laugh. It wells up in her in that old way.

Then I stop dead, just short of her noticing me. And I turn around, sun-blind, toward the empty street. I thought this woman was my mom. Crazy? Yes. Did I forget she was dead? That she wasn't as young as this woman? That those kids can't be Byron and me because—how could they be unless I'm the dead one, looking on from some greater distance than I am.

The ground lurches, and I'm still blind. And shaking like a leaf. I can hear somebody crying in another room, except here we are—I am—outdoors on a day baked into silence.

What's the real meaning of this? My mom died weeks—actually months—ago. Am I just now noticing? Hell, is Mom some item, some gym shoe I've lost at the back of my locker and didn't even miss till I came across it again by accident?

I'm sweating and crying. What have I built up all these weeks that can come crashing down on my head this quick? I'm standing on the curb of a street with some unknown name in the middle of a city I haven't actually paid much attention to. And there's nobody in sight to use or blame or lean on or anything. And I want my mother back.

The tears are all over my face, and I don't wipe them away. My hands are still clenched from gripping. And they're hanging down at my sides. I feel ape-like, grunting with grief.

I come to in stages. The first half-sane thought I have is that I'm hurting because now I'll never know my mom. Not as a person. I don't even have the option of forgetting her. I'll only remember the role she played and won't let myself remember much of that. Not at what it's costing me right now. Finally I know what *loss* means. The power of the dead is that they leave you with the living. I'm staggering under this load of new knowledge, but what do I do with it?

"Do with what?" Byron says. He's doubled back. It looks like he's walked his bike the last few feet toward me. He's standing in the curve of the handlebars, and he's squinting up at my wet face, and his eyebrows are meeting.

I reach for believable lies. I've got a flat. The gears are shot. My sprocket's sprung. They've suckered me with a defective bike.

"Why are you crying?" Byron asks, and waits.

"I'm crying about Mom," I sort of whisper. I'm so far gone that I'm telling the truth. It sounds like a foreign language.

"Oh." Byron looks down at the wet tar that snakes all over the pavement. He's half embarrassed, half something else—respectful maybe. "It's okay," he says in a small, thin voice. "I do it myself."

I can't talk. I can't let him see me like this. But he's seeing. Everything that seems to have worked for weeks grinds to a halt. The old systems are shutting down. But what I really can't do is talk around these tears. Still, I do. "I . . . really . . . need . . . you . . . a . . . lot," I say to him, wringing out every word.

"Well," he says, "sure."

I bury Mom again, less certain this time. I scatter her ashes over this subtropical street, straddle the bike, and wheel off behind Byron.

He's standing up, riding the pedals slow and easy. The wind catches in his hair, and I ride in his wake and feel it.

In a few hours, days, I settle into life with my fellow survivors. We touch up the Truce, Dad and I, and we don't bog down over petty details. We iron out some with a couple of words and walk around the rest. A little goodwill seeps in, depending on the day. We're at our best with trivia. There's even an unwritten roster for taking showers so the one left with the cold water is alternated. Byron develops a thing for cold showers, one of the big guys.

Okay, so I fire a few more zingers at Dad occasionally. Quickies, hit-and-run, sniping out of a tree. One time he gets personal, testing the future clause of the truce. He asks me what I want to be when I grow up. Rephrases by asking what I want to be when I get out of college.

"Marriage counselor," I tell him. He turns the other cheek.

Mostly I'm at my worst when I figure he's about to take Byron over, which he never quite seems to be doing. Or when I imagine Byron's drifting in his direction. After one of my verbal jabs—I forget which one—Dad says, "Take your best shot; I return fire." But he hasn't yet.

While we have our day-to-day rules, we aren't slaves to routine. The house looks pretty much the same, clean or not. If Byron should wet his bed, which he doesn't, nobody's going to rub his nose in it. We do laundry only when it's past counting. We bundle everything into a sheet: shirts, towels,

sneakers, socks, jocks—and load the Datsun down
for a trip to the laundromat.

"Boys' Town," Marietta calls our place.

"It needs a woman's touch," Dad remarks.

"Shoot, a woman wouldn't touch it," she replies.

I encounter Dad in unexpected places. Beside
his sofa bed there's a night stand/end table
magazine rack. At the bottom of a pile of paperbacks I'm browsing through, I find a heavy hard-
back volume, expensive binding, gold-stamped.

His college yearbook. With a few minutes to
myself, I leaf through this ancient document, un-
sticking its pages, and get caught up in it long before discovering Dad. There's a sort of 1950ish
centerfold of beauty queens. Big, luscious, flat,
black-and-white camera studies of retouched ice
princesses, all seeming to wear the same strapless
black dress. I know I'm not going to come suddenly upon Mom because she didn't go to this college.

So I look my fill: at Miss Beth Bartley, Delta
Delta Delta, Homecoming Queen; Miss Nancy
LeDue, Alpha Omicron Pi, May Day Queen; Miss
Elaine Lindstrom, Kappa Alpha Theta, Military
Ball Queen; Miss Alberta Cahill, Delta Zeta,
Queen of the Interfraternity Ball.

The light catches their teeth and pearls. They
smile down the years, not aging. Which I guess is
what yearbooks are for. I flash through the pages
of this forgotten world, a weird middle-earth kind
of place full of spindly halfbacks in action, cheer-
leaders doing splits, track stars with horn-rims

taped to their temples, the rifle club posing around a gun rack. Wrist corsages, debate teams, the Methodist Student Movement, a couple in incredible formal attire in an arty doorway shot, only their lips touching. It's spooky, but I like it. Everybody's smiling.

I come across Dad in the senior pictures. He's midway down an alphabetical row, but I never actually spot him. They've all got convict haircuts and clip-on bow ties, and they're all postage-stamp size.

But they've included his credentials. I read through his entry, trying to decipher it: "Atwater, Howard: Van Wert, Ohio." I try to remember his hometown, my grandparents on that side, but all I come up with is a car trip we took when I was pre-school. All I remember is a front porch with a ceiling painted sky blue and a porch swing painted green and orange.

Business Administration major. Delta Upsilon, rush chairman. ROTC. Interfraternity Council. Fresh. Soph. softball. Track mt. pep squad. Yearbook business manager. Alpha Phi Omega. Poly Sci Roundtable. Fresh. debate. Economics Club, treasurer.

It's all Greek to me, even the part that isn't. I give up on it, rebury the book under the paperbacks.

I don't snoop, but I notice Dad's got a closet full of well-seasoned fishing gear, fairly elaborate, evidently his chief possession. But he doesn't so

much as tie a fly in our presence. He hasn't taken
us fishing, or anyplace else. He's decided enter-
taining us is not the way to go. Besides, he's stuck
close to his job, sold all but two apartments in the
Barnacle Cove. He works on commission, so whatever he earns, it ebbs and flows, with dry spots.
Becoming a sudden family man may have lighted
fires under his initiative. Two more units to unload, and he'll move on to managing another building.

They'll level his house for the "subtropical
gardens and sports complex" promised in the Barnacle Cove brochure. And he'll be living somewhere else. I like the impermanence of this; it
rules out the future, enforces the truce. We're
ships passing in the fog here; a couple of hoots
from the horn, and good-bye Charlie. I lie awake
nights picturing the bulldozers coming in through
the wall, plowing the place under. Who's looking
for roots?

We've fallen into a meal routine that cuts con-
frontations to the bone. I go by myself up to
Marietta's for breakfast—the way to start a day.
Lunch is a grab bag. Byron takes an apple and a
banana and Nub into our jungle. I decide it isn't
my mission to teach him nutrition and table man-
ners. We're not running a finishing school here.
Besides, we may make it till fall; then he'll have all
the scheduling he can use.

I'd be hanging looser than I am except the
truce gets a little—weighty. On details we're
golden. But all the big issues are taboo. It's like

living in a country with perfectly workable traffic laws and no constitution.

Let Dad start playing Papa with us, and I'll nail him. But as a completely reasonable roommate, he's getting on my nerves. I'm working up to the final summer scene, when we shake hands all around at the airport (the same day they bulldoze his house) and Byron and I walk away, forgetting to get his forwarding address.

But something's already crabbing this act that I'm rehearsing. I have this nagging feeling that Dad owes us—me—some explanations. But that would involve the past, which is strictly forbidden by the famous truce authored by yours truly.

As Dad says, we're stuck with the present. The chief advantage of this present is Marietta's regular dinner-partying. We all go up to the no-name diner for a late supper every night when her evening "rush" is over and she can sit with us.

She manages to make an event out of every meal. Most nights there's something idiotic to celebrate. She sits with Byron on his side of the booth, leaving Dad and me shoulder to shoulder. She maneuvers this, refers to Byron as "the boyfriend." When he's out of his sling and eating with both hands, the two of them are very big on body contact. He's practically in her lap. The whites of his eyes glow in his berry-brown face. He's putting on weight.

"Tonight," Marietta says at one of our feasts, "we're having something special." She's explaining a carrot cake with a single candle on it, unlit. The candle reappears for various occasions. "It's

Jefferson Davis's birthday." Her violet eyes are putting us on.

"You check that out, Marietta?" I ask.

"No need," she says. And she and Dad finish in chorus: "Where I come from, every day is Jefferson Davis's birthday." Byron makes a mental note to find out who Jefferson Davis is.

"Three men," Marietta always says, her favorite saying, "equals no conversation." She builds on our truce silence, turns us into an audience, a family, whatever suits her occasion. She skates over our wordless surface effortlessly at first, executing figure eights. "When you're number nine in the Bethune family of Dothan, Alabama," she says (often), "you've heard a power of conversation in your time."

Then she returns to her favorite theme, the great day coming when she'll steal Mr. Got-Rocks away from Mrs. Got-Rocks and "be sassier than a born-again C.B.er."

"You know where I'll live when I'm the second Mrs. Got-Rocks?" She digs Byron in the ribs. He's all funny bones, Marietta notes. He's developing a giggle, rising out of a gurgle. He's halfway to a belly laugh. It's only days away. We all know where Marietta will live in her fantasy future. Palm Beach she's never seen, so it's to be Coral Gables.

Byron and I have biked all over Coral Gables, which lies off Coconut Grove's flank, in a different world. An upper-crust suburb on a wrought-iron and pink plaster theme with banyan boulevards and mansions backed up to their own yacht canals.

"I'll be stretched out there on my shez long," Marietta predicts, "and even them little spaces between my toes will have the best tan you ever seen. And I'll have a butler to bring me out my lunch on a tray—a little butler, cute and Cuban. Your size." She elbows Byron.

But the real Marietta breaks through the dream. "And I'll have me a garden run right to the street with a border of quartz rocks. Spearmint for iced tea, garlic for salads, beefsteak tomatoes, mushmelons, pie squash, peanuts, roast nears." We all have to work on this last crop. It becomes roasting ears, which translates to corn on the cob.

"And"—she scans us—"I'm going to set aside one night a week out of my busy social schedule to entertain Yankees."

"We'll come," Byron says, totally taken in. The fact that we're all three in love with her, revolve around her, spurs her on to greater heights. We're her groupies.

But questions start to form in her eyes, even when her own conversation is flowing free. Half our weirdness she puts down to Yankee ways. She sees we're not a family, not in her definition of the word. But she's too careful, too kind to ask us why not.

"My daddy," she says, pulling him out of the air, "whoooeee, you didn't want to put your tail across the line with him! Whuppin' for one was whuppin' for all. Had him an old Harley-Davidson and tore up the slab with it. But Sundays? We took up a whole pew, and my daddy'd boom out them hymns—'I Come to the Garden Alone' and 'Still, Still with Thee, When Purple Morning Breaketh'—till you couldn't hear yourself pray.

"Whooooeee," she says softly, shaking her head at me, not thinking about her daddy at all, wondering instead why I don't want one.

Sundays, her day off, she spends with us. Yes, the flowered bikini in my drawer is hers. She changes in my room. I don't care how long the bikini's been there. Now is what counts.

She never goes in the pool, hasn't been near water since she "was throwed in the branch" by her brother Peadell.

We don't believe anybody's named Peadell. "What's his real name, Marietta?"

"I told you—Peadell. You don't want to hear his nickname."

She never tans. Well, only a little. When she sits with arms locking her knees, there's a curving wedge of paler skin just beneath her bikini. Her waist is child-small, and her legs are twice as long as they seem behind her apron. She could be the center fold-out for *Farmer's Almanac*. Following the sun that hardly touches her, she migrates around the pool. She never wears sunglasses, only an old straw gardening hat that must have come down from Dothan with her. That hat band features a repeating pattern of Confederate flags.

I unfurl a beach towel next to her. But I don't move every times she does. I'm cautious, never want to hear the term "puppy love" from her lips. When I pull myself out of the pool—Mark Spitz without medals—Dad has zeroed in. They're lying side by side on their stomachs, talking quietly into their towels. They slip back in time, shifty as teenagers, into a pre-summer pattern I don't think about.

I pretend to be bushed by the pool workout and lie with heaving chest on the concrete watching them through squinting eyes. Blue veins in knots stand out on the backs of Dad's legs. Blue spiders on the ankles, branching blue road-map lines up over the calves, bulging blue worms massed behind his knees. He's too old for her. There are a thousand proofs of this. I have the entire thousand filed alphabetically, ready to pull. He's got a *daughter* who's not that much younger than Marietta, for Lord's sake. Funny how Lorraine never happens to come up in conversation. I earmark an item in my mental file. In Florida it's tough staying uptight, but I find ways.

Byron's become an expert back-floater. He drifts all over the pool; deep end, shallow end, it's all the same to him. And he has the buoyancy of an inner tube. Also, he's developing a small potbelly. With skinny legs trailing, he floats at the surface like some cartoon jellyfish, deaf to the world behind the ear plugs I make him wear.

We've been looking for a reason to celebrate, dine out in style on Sunday night at the Coco Plum. It's near enough Bastille Day, though Marietta points out that they don't observe this in Dothan. And the Coco Plum specialty is crepes. So this decides it. We'll eat French pancakes to celebrate the French Revolution, and Marietta won't have to cook.

We gather up the towels. Byron staggers up the shallow-end steps, doing his Creature from the Black Lagoon number and popping out his plugs. We're halfway down the path when Marietta says to him, "Where's that ole cat you used to have?"

"Oh, he's gone," Byron says, twirling the underwater goggles he always brings to the pool and never wears.

Dad and I exchange glances, for the first time. We're both thinking the same thing, both trying to remember the last time we saw Nub. And can't. Subliminal Nub. Deadweight Nub. Moron-king of the refrigerator top, never caught up on his sleep. Memory's beginning to serve us. Nobody's kicked over Nub's milk bowl in a week. Nobody's found a fur ball, shimmering like a slug, in the sink. Nobody's discovered a flattened Tender Vittle stuck into a sneaker tread lately.

"What do you mean he's gone, Byron?" Dad puts a hand out, reining him in. "Is he lost?"

Oh, great, he's lost his cat, and he's wrecked by it, and nobody noticed. Except, of course, Marietta.

"Why didn't you tell us?" Dad says. We have a crisis here. Marietta senses it even though house pets don't play a big role in her background. She has the universal look of somebody who's just put her foot in something.

"It's okay," Byron says, watching the goggles flashing around his finger. We're standing in the scaled-down jungle, and I picture Nub eaten by hyenas or smeared halfway to Homestead on the Dixie Highway. "He likes it outdoors," Byron's explaining in a let's-not-make-a-big-deal tone. "I'd take him out, and he really liked the woods. First he went up a tree after a bird and fell down. But up he went again. I never saw him get a bird, but he caught a mouse—or something like a mouse. When I saw, he'd eaten most of it. Maybe he didn't really catch it, but he ate it. There are raccoons out here, too, tame enough to come up for handouts. Nub would dance around them, not too close, but he liked them. He goes after lizards too—those little gray ones like dinosaurs."

Still, we stand on the path, wondering how to take this. "But you put out water and cat food for him, don't you?" I say. "You want him to come back? You don't want to lose him?"

Byron shakes his head, not needing this attention. "He's gone back to nature." His head swivels around at the trees. "He knows where water is out here. And he finds food. Cats are hunters," he explains. "Oh, one night he came back and jumped up on my windowsill and looked in. But when I came to the screen, he jumped off and went back in the woods. He was just checking on me. He's an animal. He likes being free."

The evening sort of falls apart. Why am I not glad to have Nub out from underfoot? Why is it I'd rather see Byron upset about this? The damn cat was the only thing that was ever completely his own. It wasn't some toy he'd gotten tired of and gradually outgrown. He'd actually trained

Nub to be independent and then watched him creep away, back to nature.

Dad's looking rattled too, which I don't mind nearly so much.

Somehow the Coco Plum plan peters out. Marietta warms up canned chili, miraculously finds cayenne powder at the back of our kitchen cupboard. We eat in cereal bowls, with oyster crackers, sweet dills, divvy up some sherbert from the refrigerator's freezer. It's not an event, but we eat.

"I raised a piglet from a runt one time," Marietta says, re-inventing conversation. "Bottle-fed him up to where you wouldn't know him, and let him sleep in a drawer behind the stove. Course you know what happened when he come of age. . . ."

"Bacon," Byron says, scooping up a mittful of oyster crackers.

"Chitlins," Marietta adds.

"Ham sandwiches," Byron counters.

"Pickled pig's feet," Marietta concludes. They start giggling. Dad looks at me, raises his eyes, lifts his shoulders. Crisis past.

Eleven

This August morning starts out like a full-color production number. It's a day like no other days. The air's full of promises. Rain in the night and thunder in the bay. Water's still plopping off the palm leaves. My room's full of washed green shadows. It's almost cool.

I arise . . . aroused. I've been dreaming of Marietta or some fantastic country-and-Western starlet cast in her part. All night this figure from Central Casting has lounged dreamlike around the pool in Marietta's bikini. No, truth to tell, she's wearing less than that. The details return in the dawn. My number on the cold-shower roster has come up, and I'm a prime candidate.

I do a little barefoot soft-shoe shuffle to the shower, throw my head back and gargle the ice water, expect great things from the stretching-ahead day. Then heat kitchen-kettle water for a careful shave to crown my mood. Stride from room to room buck-naked, feeling mildly X-rated.

Swimming laps is paying off. A hint of definition is peeking through under the pects. My shoulders don't quite fit into the shaving mirror. Maybe they never did, but today I notice. I lather up face, chin, overdoing it somewhat. I let the razor bite back my sideburns a half inch—the only serious shaving the razor has to do. Stare into the bubbly mirror in search of emerging image. Do things you do only in a mirror: flare a nostril, cock an eye, consider contrast between teeth and tan, create an actual part in my hair and slick it down like a hopeful Princeton freshman.

Lorraine's letter is discovered on the counter where I've been walking my bobbing manhood back and forth past it a half a dozen trips. The letter looks like it's crossed the Atlantic in a bottle. Forwarded from Brooklyn Heights, then from Grandmother at the Buck Hill Falls Inn, then on to me. Little does Lorraine know where her letter has finally washed up. Would she go all soft and mushy to learn Byron and Dad and I are reunited under a single roof? Only if she knew.

She's had her baby; this is the announcement. Nine and a half pounds, a mere nothing, given Lorraine's size. "The whole birth was easy as falling off a log," Lorraine writes. A terrible image, terrorizing even, if you take it literally. But then Lorraine was not a Creative Writing major. They've named it—him—Carl because he was born in Germany. Could be a lot worse: Rudolph. Siegfried. Wolfgang. Her writing sprawls

all over the airmail page. Is she writing while lying down or falling off a log? No, this is the way
she writes. X's for kisses to Byron and me and
threats of baby pictures to follow.

I check the postmark. Lorraine's baby is already three weeks old. It's August already. The
endless summer takes a lurch forward.

I stick the letter in my shirt pocket, under the
alligator emblem. I haven't figured out a use for
this letter, or why it should have one. I head up
the path to the pool, meaning to inform Byron of
his uncledom.

What I find is beeper-belted Dad giving him a
pool-side haircut. A light trim, but close contact.
Byron's sitting on a deck chair footrest, draped in
a beach towel. Dad's squatting down, snipping
away. I let this pass in the name of economy.
There's no point in throwing dollars away on such
monotonies as haircuts. I let them off with a
wave, and cut around past the grand entrance of
the Barnacle Cove on the way to breakfast. The
concrete canopy over the front drive is already developing liver spots from the damp. Dad had better unload the last unit in this turkey before it
falls down.

Even downtown Coconut Grove is astir in this
magic morning. There's a version of autumn in
the air. The tourist season, wonderful warm
make-a-buck winter, is only weeks away. The girl
and the guy who run the Levis-n-Tops Shop are
out on the sidewalk, up and down a ladder.
They're fitting a new awning over the store-front.
Midnight blue with white fringe and tassels be-

tween the scallops. Upgrading from funky to chic. The Grove's showing signs of making a giant leap forward from the Sixties to the Eighties. Time is still ticking, after all.

"What-a-ya think, man?" the guy says from the ladder top, running ringed hands over expensive blue canvas. I don't even know these people, but it's that kind of morning.

"Far out," I say, in his language. "Class."

"That's the look we're looking for," he says down to me. He can't keep his hands off the canvas. His bib overalls are tapered, flared, maybe lined with Hong Kong silk.

Marietta's counter is full. A solid row of work-shirt backs and elbows. She's working them like an assembly line. Sends me a high sign with the hand that isn't pouring coffee. I can wait. She's still last night's dream, fully clothed, aproned. On a paper napkin I do elementary math. When I'm, say, fifty-eight, she'll be sixty-four—sixty-five tops.

I'm not taking this computation to heart. I just like the mental gymnastics of telescoping time. I like the way our lives overlap with loose ends. If she and I were the same age, she'd be hundreds of miles away—wherever Dothan, Alabama, is—getting ready for senior year. Simmering in a summer of kudzu vines, picket fences, hollyhocks growing right up to the slab, cheerleader clinics, drag races. She'd be ringing up sweet milk and groceries at U-Tote-M with some pimply sacker slobbering all over her. Her added years draw us together, keeping the Real Me a dark secret from both of us. The real me being a male virgin wallflower in a nervous knot of fellow sufferers—put Kit Klein in there—sweating out a Van Cortlandt/Spence mixer.

The work shirts rise in a body—a chorus line of construction boots—give Marietta one last leer, pay up, poke the toothpick dispenser, and shuffle out.

"Street crew," she says, bearing down on me with her bottomless coffeepot. "They're patching the slab on Ingraham Road this morning. Keep me on the hop while they're here, but they all leave at once, thank the Lord."

"Good tippers?" I inquire.

"Better be," she says, suddenly shrewd again, "if they want lunch where they had breakfast."

"I like watching you work," I say. This has meaning. I like watching her *breathe*, and I don't just mean the rise and fall of those apple breasts behind the blouse. But working, she's—poetry in motion. I don't say all this, of course.

"Story of my life," Marietta says. "Men never tire of watching women work." But she gets my drift. When she reaches across to pull the sugar bowl my way, I go for it at the same time. I'm working on my timing. My hand covers hers for a moment. She gives me one of her you're-quite-a-little-guy smiles. I'm very anxious to establish the distinction in her mind between me and Byron.

"Come on," she says. "Got something to show you."

"Can't." I shake my head. "I'm stuck in this booth."

She draws me out, her hand closing lightly over my wrist. We thread our way out back through the kitchen I've never seen, past the cook who never looks up—a hobbit in a paper cap, feeding potatoes into the jaws of a mechanical peeler. Outside the screen door is a back yard, sealed off from the street. In a sun-baked el between the diner and another shacklike structure Marietta's created a garden.

"I just putter out here when I get a chance," she says, downgrading the very place she's brought me out to see, to share.

It's not Brooklyn Botanic Garden. It's . . . something else. The night rain has washed it clean, laid its dust. The whitewalls on the tires she's planted flower beds in are snow circles. She's lined a path with pop bottles, necks planted in the sandy soil. A double row of green and brown bottle bottoms puddle the sun, divide the path from straggly cactus, ferns, mostly plain dirt. Institutional-size fruit cocktail cans hold potted palms.

"Nothing I'm used to wants to grow down here," she says. "I take no credit for the hibiscus." The hibiscus that grows all over Florida is in full yellow and red flower. It pays no attention to Marietta's plan, sprawls, tries to scale fences into parking lots. She's built a birdbath out of a piano stool topped with a blue enamel wash basin. It stands in a circle of crushed shells. Past it, against the woven-wire fence, the end of the garden, is her single piece of lawn furniture—a buckled bench that was once a diner booth. "Oh, one of these times I'll have me a real garden," she says. "White wrought-iron furniture. A shez long."

She's—we're—thinking of her Coral Gables garden, but this isn't the place to mention it. She nips a hibiscus blossom from the fence and plants it behind her ear. Red and classy against her black hair.

We sit on the bench, our legs in the sun. She rests her feet, props rubber heels in the white crushed shells. She's shared her garden with me, and I have just enough sense not to praise it. She'd put down my praise. I take her hand, and we lace fingers, rest them on the bench between us. I'm back in last night's dream without the big anxieties. We're brother and sister.

My mind goes to Lorraine's letter in my pocket, but the sun's stunning me. Still, I finally manage to break the spell. I'm at my best in ruining good things.

"Where do you live, Marietta?" I never even wondered before.

"Right here in this garden if I could," she murmurs. Her eyes are shut against the sun. She stirs herself. "Right now I'm staying with a girl over on Seminole. We're two to a room, but she works nights."

"Sounds like close quarters."

"Believe it."

"Why don't you get out?"

"Might do that."

"When?" (Why am I pushing this? Maybe she can't *afford* her own place, for God's sake.)

"One of these times. End of the summer maybe," she says.

My mind skips a beat, followed by a flash of lightning. I'm not the only one sitting out the summer. She's waiting for Byron and me to leave, and then she'll move in with Dad. Or more likely—the bikini in the drawer—she'll be moving back in with him after this annoying interruption.

The Hardy Boy has reconstructed the crime. The puzzle piece falls into place beneath his unerring hand. After a bit of fiddling with the knobs, we have a clear picture here.

My hand, not too steady, goes up to Lorraine's letter. "I heard from my sister today," I hear myself saying. I've pulled my other hand away from Marietta's, needing both to open the envelope my sweat has sealed again. I wait, to hear if she knows I have a sister.

"She the one married to the soldier boy?" She knows.

"Air Force."

"How's she doing?" I offer her the letter, but she looks away. She doesn't read other people's mail.

"She's had a baby," I say. This is the big punch line. How come I didn't know?

Marietta sits up, draws in her feet, smiles the first real smile of the day—pure pleasure. "What she have?" Now she's almost capable of taking the letter off me.

"A boy."

"Nice!" She settles back into a reverie of talcum powder, Pampers, bassinets. I see her seeing a crib with a big blue bow on it and a dangling mobile. Small baby feet doing high kicks. Somehow this isn't the direction I want her going in.

"What'd your daddy have to say about that!" Her teeth catch her lower lip in a smile to coax all kinds of warm, sentimental tidbits from me.

"I didn't tell him."

Her smile fades, and there's puzzlement clouding her eyes. "Why not? You seen him yet this morning?"

"Saw him, but didn't tell him."

"You mean you didn't tell him he's a grandpa?" I can feel her wonder without looking.

"Yeah," I mumble. "Think about it. He's a grandpa."

She doesn't think about it. "He'll bust his buttons when he hears! You better scoot along home and tell him."

"Look, Marietta, I'm Jim, not Byron. I walk. Sometimes I jog. I've been known to break into a run. But I don't scoot."

"Well, whatever. . . ," she says, mystified, drawing back.

"The point is, Marietta, your—my dad is a grandfather. Get it?"

"I got it first time around."

I should hang it up right now. I should scoot along home. It's going to be all downhill from here on. But no, I haven't made my point. "Marietta, he's a grandfather. He's too old for—skip it.

Forget it." Still I don't get up and scoot out of this found-art garden while the scooting's good.

Marietta's shifted on the bench, studying me. But I'm concentrating on my feet digging furrows in the white shells she's put there. "My daddy was thirty-nine first time he was a grandpa," she says softly.

"Yeah, well, your daddy wasn't making it with a chick half his age at the time, I assume." The morning flies apart in fragments. I have wasted it, in the worst meaning of that word.

The minute I've said it, I don't believe it myself. I want to reach up in the air and pull the words back, jam them back down my throat.

Marietta sits unmoving, her eyes on me. Then reaches up and takes the hibiscus flower out of her hair, turns the stem in her hand. Puts it down on the bench and then brushes it off on the ground.

"Well, I ought to be getting back," she says. "I've stayed out here too long as it is." She starts to go.

"No, don't," I say. I'm sick to my stomach. I'm sick of myself.

"I don't take it personal," Marietta says, softer than before. "I know you're out to spite your daddy, not me. That's your burden, not mine." Then she's moving around the birdbath and along the bottle path, away from the snake in her Eden. The screen door snaps shut behind her.

I have to follow her. I have no place else to go. Crazy Louise, the beachcombing shopping-bag lady, is the only customer in the diner. She's helped herself to coffee, sits at the far end of the counter in her mountain of rags, gumming the rim of the mug. So Marietta and I are still as good as alone.

She's already behind the counter, mopping up under a cake stand, nothing in her face. I straddle the nearest stool, scared she'll move away. "I'm sorry," I say. I've never been sorrier in my life.

"I am too," she says. And I know she means she's sorry for me.

"I don't even believe it."

"What?"

"What I said."

"I don't understand," Marietta says, the rag in her hand making wet arcs on the counter, "but the worst sin in your book is somebody loving your daddy. It doesn't seem natural." She shakes her head at this—perversion. "If your mama hadn't loved your daddy, you wouldn't even be here." She folds the wet rag in on itself.

"Your mama died last spring, didn't she?"

"Yeah, she—"

"Never mind. She died."

"That's right," Crazy Louise says down the counter. But she's not following this. She hears voices in her head and answers back.

"I never mentioned your mama," Marietta says. "Where I come from people comfort each other—with words. But I knew the first time your daddy brought you boys in here that wasn't your way. I didn't know what to make of you. Didn't know if you were too grieved to feel or too unfeeling to grieve. So I did what I could to make you all feel better about things. Every night I did my poor best—in that booth right over there.

"You think I didn't know I was playing mama for three lost souls? You used me for that. You most of all. I already knew your daddy. Passing time with his boys was only natural. Lord knows he didn't seem to know how to handle you himself. And Byron—anybody'd take pity on a little child floundering around and solemn with it. So that leaves you. And now, today, you've repaid me."

"That's right," Crazy Louise mutters. "You can't deny a thing like that."

I've got my head down now. I'm crying, mostly inside.

"You scoo—go on home now," Marietta says, as quietly as if Crazy Louise really could understand. "I won't let on. It'll be like before. We'll finish out the summer, and there's no sense in raising sand and showing ill feeling with Byron around. You're not the only one who can use him as an excuse for doing and not doing."

I'm at the door then, half blind. I can't find the knob. My hand fights the cord on the blind. I can't get out of here quick enough, and I can't get out. "Jim?" she calls over. She's got her customer smile on; she's back in business. "Remember what I said first. I don't take it too personal. But listen here, sport"—she gives her mopping-up rag a playful little whip-crack in the air—"if I was your mama, I'd tan your bottom!"

I try to smile back. She makes a face at this pathetic effort. "And I'm old enough to be your mama too, believe it."

I'm pretty much past believing anything. I just stare at her.

"I'm thirty," she calls out, "thirteen years older than you. Where I come from that's old enough to be your mama!"

"That's right," Crazy Louise cackles. "There aren't two ways about it."

Twelve

There are no holes to crawl into. Living through
the day, of course, is not a reasonable option. It's
stretching to infinity, and we're talking about
eleven o'clock in the morning. I could possibly
live till noon, but not with myself.

I think about rounding up Byron. Anybody
who floats that well should learn a good breast-
stroke, a dog paddle anyhow. In a couple of weeks
I could have him diving off the high board. I
could ... leave him alone.

I happen to know he's collecting lizards, his favorite dinosaur variety. I happen to know he's
got a sneaker box under his bed full of lizards on
lettuce leaves, like a weird salad. He studies them
every night and turns them loose in the mornings
and collects a new batch to study or play with or
room with or whatever. A private occupation.

I know if I stand much longer at the intersec-

tion of McFarlane and Grand looking wrecked,
some public-spirited pedestrian is going to call
the paramedics to come for me.

I head for the Barnacle Cove—not our back lot
but the high rise with the liver spots and the gen-
uine bronze aluminum window frames. Busy as
my morning has been, I haven't worked through
the agenda. One thing leads to another, and there
are no instant replays. Going back to explain to
Marietta that we live in a laid-back age when
words don't really mean anything is out. Because
where she comes from . . .

Saving the day is not on the agenda.

The "uniformed-doorman-standing-at-attention-
under-the-canopy," who's promised in the brochure, hasn't appeared yet. Possibly he hasn't even
been born yet. I walk through the full-security
doors and into the lobby. It's furnished with a
color drawing of how it's going to look furnished.
I walk across crumbling concrete sub-flooring to a
button labeled *Ring for Manager to View Model
Apartments.*

I ring. The grille above the button speaks in
Dad's voice. He's upstairs. "Would you like to see
the apartment?" his robot voice asks, tinny
through static.

"Yeah," I say, possibly not in my right voice.

"Third floor. Turn right out of the elevator."

I've never been inside the Barnacle Cove before. The full blast of air conditioning feels wet
on my face. In a complete transfusion real air is
efficiently sucked away and replaced by sheer

crispness. In this vacuum I'm about to have a word with Dad.

One doorway's open. I step inside into an entrance lined in aluminum-foil wallpaper. The place is decorated to death with electric-blue carpeting, white plaster table lamps shaped like palm trees, nubby white sofas on silver ball castors, and mirrored walls to double the room size. With the silver, blue, and white geometrics on screens, it's Dr. Zhivago's ice palace as assembled by a department store.

Dad steps out of the bedroom which is his office. "Good—"

"Morning," I finish, to cover his surprise. I'm standing there in the middle of the room, electric-blue carpeting nibbling at my sneakers, my hands planted in my back pockets.

He's standing in the doorway, rumpled but receptive. "Thought I had a customer," he says, questions standing out all over him. "Interested?" he says. "Make you a deal you can't refuse—eighty-nine five, no closing, no hidden fees. Throw in health-club membership to the right buyer."

I scan the room, glad for a role to play. "Only if you decorate."

We stand there on this neutral ground, kind of smirking at each other, groping for a beginning.

"Come on into my—office," he says finally. In there folding chairs crowd around a banged-up pine office desk, the only sticks of furniture in the place built for human use. Teetering piles of brochures carry banner headlines: THE BARNACLE COVE: THE ELEGANCE THAT BECOMES YOU.

"Catchy," I say, jerking a thumb at the slogan. "Deft double meaning."

"The advertising agency wanted to put it on T-shirts," he says. His eyes scan the ceiling to mock Madison Avenue. And then he fires a random shot. "Speaking of T-shirts, what slogan would you have on yours right now?"

I don't even have to think. I'm practically pulling it on over my head as we speak. "BORN TO BOMB OUT."

He considers this.

"And you?"

He considers this too, then nods. "Nothing too witty. I think—I HOPE I CAN SWIM BECAUSE I'M OUT OF MY DEPTH."

We gravitate to chairs, opposite each other across the desk. Buyer and seller? Patient and doctor? Repulsive brat sent to the headmaster's office?

"Why is it," Dad says, "that I have this feeling you're offering me your head on a platter?"

"I think I've already cut my own throat," I say.

"At the risk of speaking in a father's voice," he says, genuinely cautious, "do you want to talk about it?"

"I don't think I've got much choice."

"First of all," he says, "does this touch on the past, the future, or certain people we're not supposed to mention?"

"No. But screw the truce."

"The Lord giveth and the Lord taketh away," he says. I have this coming. I am the Lord.

"I've—messed up with Marietta."

"Messed up?"

"I've insulted her."

He's got his fingertips pressed together again. He's staring into them. I think he is—I don't know. My head's almost between my knees, level with the desk. Sulking again—you don't kick these habits overnight.

"So at last you've found out about Marietta," he says, which bring me around.

"Found out what?"

"That she's a human being in her own right, and nobody's easy convenience."

"You're making this too easy."

"I can make it easier. I've been there," he says. "The first night I walked into the diner, I made a pass at her."

"And?"

"I've been turned down before, but she gave the experience an entirely new meaning. She has this way of looking right through you, cutting you off at the knees, and then smiling you out the door."

He's been there all right.

"It took me a solid year to get back in her good graces."

"Then what?"

He raises his eyebrows the way he does when he's stating the obvious. "By then I was in love with her." He's even willing to close the case without a cross-examination. He knows I've taken my lumps.

Here we are man-to-man: incredible confrontation. And the room feels full of women. Marietta, Lorraine, hints of Grandmother, Mom.

Lorraine. I go for her letter in my pocket, find I've lost it.

"Lorraine's letter?" asks Dad, this all-seeing wizard. "I left it for you on the counter."

"Yeah. She's had a baby. A boy."

Into the quiet that follows this, he says, "You're full of news this morning."

"She wonders how you feel about it."

"Lorraine? How could she—"

"No. Marietta." He's linking up both my news items. I see it in his face.

"How do I feel?" he asks. "I'm a grandfather—remote, but still a grandfather. And how do I feel? I don't know. It comes too soon after being a father."

"You've had a summer's worth of that," I say.

"No, I'm having about ten minutes' worth of that."

We decide to go out looking for Byron, last seen on his hands and knees in a jungle playing ringmaster for a lizard circus. We're suspending conversation on a high—an unparalleled—peak for us. We're practically capable of slapping each other on the back. We've expanded physically. We can barely get through the door. We're also not pushing our luck.

Byron's where last seen. His rump in trunks is sticking up along the path halfway between the pool and our house. It's a well-known fact that you can't go near those little gray-beige lizards. They move at the speed of light, beyond the hand of man. One of them is climbing over Byron's wrist. Four more are peering out of weeds at him, ready to do his bidding. He's cleared a circle of dirt and is trying a diet on them: lettuce, radish bits, something that looks like Granola.

He sees us with the eyes in the back of his head. "Stay behind me. I've about got this one tame."

We do as we're told. "Can we talk?" I say, not wanting to disturb Byron's balance of nature.

"Yeah. They're deaf, I think. What are you guys doing?"

"We—ah—just wanted to tell you Lorraine's had her baby," Dad says. "A boy." It's difficult to talk to the back of a lizard trainer.

"Oh," Byron says. "It takes nine months, doesn't it." He's not angling for information.

"Yes," Dad says.

"Then I guess the nine months is up," Byron says. "This one's missing part of its tail."

Dad and I exchange looks. Our shoulders lift simultaneously. "Let's have a beer," he says.

"To celebrate?" I don't say what.

"No, let's just have a beer." We execute a wide circle around Byron into Nub's jungle and head off down to the house.

I ease up on the counter top, let my legs dangle. I'm loose as a goose. I've been low. I've been high. Now I don't know where I am. Dad pops tops, hands me a can, climbs on the stool. "Jesus," he says, looking up, "you're almost a man."

"Almost," I say. "Worst word in the tongue. Almost human. Almost scored. Almost made it."

"Almost missed out completely," he adds, turning the word.

"What am I going to do about Marietta?" I say.

"You're going to leave Marietta to me."

"You'll be in good hands. You going to marry her?"

"No," he says, into his beer. "I'm not the marrying kind, remember?"

Beautiful. I'd have to admire it even against my will, even in the heat of battle. Now he's the one offering his head on a platter. To me. But we're past that. I'm pretty sure we're at the outer limits now. "About Mom," I say.

Maybe this is too much. Maybe this is beyond the limits. Suddenly I can't remember her before she was sick. A blank appears where her face should be, just when I look Dad in the eye. Having them both was never in the cards, but here I am dealing out a new hand.

"Go on," he says. "It's all right."

"Why did you lea—why couldn't the two of you make it?" This is ridiculous. Like this is the only divorce on record, like I've never heard of such an incredible thing before.

He's studying the can in his hand. But he's still there with me. I study the furrows in his forehead.

"I can't come up with one specific reason. Settle for a shortcut?"

I'd settle for less than that—nothing—if that's

the way he wants it. I can't say all this. I've probably said too much. I'm getting verbal as hell.

"We started too early," he says, giving each word weight.

"Didn't everybody get married early when you were . . ."

"Young," Dad finishes. "But we had an extra incentive."

"Not Grandmother," I say, a first instance of using Grandmother to lighten the tone.

"No," he says, dead serious, "not your grandmother. Lorraine."

Byron would grasp this quicker than I do. But I grasp it. They had to get married. I make a lunge to defend Mom's honor and find she's gone.

"Later," Dad's saying, "much later, it was too easy for me to walk away from a situation I could say I never really wanted. She—your mother—had someplace to go, back with your grandmother. I knew you'd all be taken care of, and that was all the excuse I needed. I know now how gutless that was. But if I had it to do over, I can't say I wouldn't do the same thing, because I don't know."

I sit there, thinking over the beginning and the end of this marriage which I don't even take personally. I slosh beer around in the can. It seems a great opportunity to keep my mouth shut.

"You're waiting to hear more, aren't you?" he says.

"No. I'm waiting for you to tell me if I had a few more years on me and some more experience I'd be able to understand it all."

"Never crossed my mind. It's not the kind of thing I'd particularly like to hear myself," he says. And then, "Reach backward, behind you, the drawer under the knives."

I lean back, grope down the counter to the second drawer. Peer over my own shoulder as I yank it out. It's full of curled snapshots. "Pick one at random."

I pick three that are stuck together, this being Florida. What do we have here? Half-familiar scenes. The first one is Lorraine in her high-school cap and gown, gripping her diploma from the Birch Wathen School. She's standing in the little Birch Wathen cloister garden, filling it up. Another is me, Prospect Park setting, the year before acne. I'm leaning on a ball bat that comes up to my elbow. Another one of me and Byron; he's pre-school. We're facing the camera like a firing squad, kid-like, against a wall. It could be any wall, but I think it's Grandmother's garage. I don't even remember the picture-taking, just details. Lorraine's cap and gown, Byron's sweat shirt, which is one of my old ones. "These are all after you left."

He nods.

"Did Mom—"

"No, after the split there was nothing. Well, lawyers, and then nothing. Grace—your grandmother—kept in touch. An occasional report, couple of lines at the most. Maybe twice a year and no replies to my replies."

"But why?"

Dad shrugged. "I'm not sure I know. Except

that she has a very orderly—moral sense. I may have been on her conscience, slightly. She'd never liked me. We got off on the wrong foot. She may have thought she'd made it harder for me to stay and easier for me to go than if she hadn't been looming in the background, ready to take you over in the end.

"I never questioned it. I wanted those reports and the pictures."

He's staring into the refrigerator door and rubbing his chin with the back of his hand. Then he pulls himself together. Complete mood change. Tilts the stool back, hooks his thumb in a belt loop. "What I would like—Jesus, I forgot my beeper—what I would like is for you to meet a girl and take her out. You've been in a monastery all summer."

"Longer than that," I say.

"Longer than *this summer*? Damn!" Faking amazement that anything could be longer than what we've been through.

"A girl," I say, "is no farther away than that telephone." My hand sweeps out into the room. I nearly fall off my perch. It's possible that I'm half drunk on a half can of beer.

"You're talking long distance," Dad says. "You're talking New York."

"I'm talking about a single message unit on a local call."

"Who is she, not that I doubt you."

"Her name is . . . Adele Parker. I wrote it down on a boarding pass, complete with phone number. She's a fox. I met her on the plane coming down."

"And you haven't called her before?"

I fiddle with the beer can. "Before, Marietta kept my . . . fantasies fairly well fulfilled." Dad looks my way, and we share the sheepishness.

"You say you met her on the plane? Fast worker."

"Actually Byron took care of all that. You see, he figured her for a stowaway and took it on himself to cover for her and—"

"Stop." Dad's grinning. "I've heard enough." We lob beer cans from immense distance into a Winn-Dixie shopping bag.

Thirteen

I wait till I have the house alone to dial Adele Parker's number, ring her bells. Confidence ebbs: the number's familiar, but I can't place the face.

Finally the phone's answered, twice. "Hello?" followed by a click. Adele's voice, probably, but a Mystery Guest on an extension. Will the real Adele Parker please stand up? "I've got it, *Mother*," Adele says. There's not another click, though. Mother's hanging in there.

I introduce myself again; my voice cracks for the first time in three years. "Jim Atwater!" I roar, like I'm leading cheers. Because I have this trouble saying my own name. Always have; I've stopped worrying about it. "The plane down . . . my little brother . . . a cat . . ."

Enough. She remembers. She's pleasant but guarded. Maybe she wonders what took me so long. Chooses her words with care because we're playing to an audience on this call.

After some slow-moving chitchat we both say, "Would you like—" Politely I pull back. Ladies first. I don't know what I was going to ask her to do anyway. Haven't laid the groundwork.

"—to come over here?" she says.

"Tonight?" I say, rushing my fences and wanting an excuse not to eat at Marietta's—not tonight.

Yes, tonight. I hear the monotony of months in Adele's voice. It's been a long summer. "Come on over any time. I don't eat dinner."

The extension catches its breath. Definitely her mother, scandalized at Adele's telling a stranger that proper nutrition is not practiced in that household. Dead giveaway. Adele provides address and directions. Desperate for company. Why do I regard this as a put-down instead of an opportunity? Why do I spend every minute while talking to a girl asking myself questions? "Bring your trunks," Adele says.

I go on my bike at the first sign of evening. Trunks, towel, deodorant squeeze bottle for *après*-swim, in flight bag dangling on a handlebar. By following directions, I leave Coconut Grove behind and sail into Coral Gables, pumping hard on the approaches to humpback bridges over yacht canals—touch of old Venice. I zip down boulevards blacked out by banyans, past lime-green, tangerine, French-gray houses sprawling on lawns with little cast-iron hitching-post boys by the drives. Carriage lamps wink encouragement.

I'm past Cremona, Sistina, Paradiso—grand boulevards all—when I'm nearly totaled by a Porsche that comes from behind out of nowhere and rockets past me into the night. I wobble on and arc into the Parkers' driveway. This must be the place. The street numbers are back-lighted at the curb and appear again on Portuguese tiles up by the front door.

The whole place is blazing with electricity. There's a small spotlight under every palm tree and big fake torches flanking the ironwork gates over the front door. I find a parking place for my bike in the three-lanes-wide drive, which is completely floodlit.

And walk between two metal boxes, where the curving path begins, which seem to trigger six or eight more invisible lights pinpointed around the lawn. It's like Christmas in New Jersey.

I press the (illuminated) doorbell, but the front door behind the iron grille is already opening and a slinky figure is coming into view. I have my smile of recognition at half mast.

And flash it full in the face of a middle-aged woman. Palm-frond shadows across her face. A hand extends to the gate lock, but doesn't turn it. "Friend of . . ."

"Adele's," I say, giving the password. She glances down at my flight bag.

"Ah, yes, Jim . . ."

"Atwater."

"I'm her mother." The hand blazing with diamonds springs the lock. She's wearing a long orange terry-cloth—thing. Her hair, familiar au-

burn, is waved over one eye. She has a terminal
tan, beginning to checker. A very attractive croc-
odile.

"We have to be so careful," she says, and plants
the hand on her hollow chest. "The things you
hear about . . ." She turns a hand in the air.
"Come in. Adele's dying to see you." She looks at
me over one shoulder. "Or is that the thing to
say?" I haven't a clue.

She whisks me inside, still eyeing the flight
bag. I swing it a little to indicate the absence of
heavy weaponry. Still, I could have a length of
wire, two gags, and a knife in there. Her eyes
aren't satisfied. She closes the door behind us. It's
got locks all the way to the floor, New York style.
"So careful," she says. And leads me on across tile
and into carpet country.

The room is so big it has furniture in the
middle of it, like an island in a beige sea. Beyond
that, through sliding glass doors, is a walled pool
the width of the house, lighted bright blue from
beneath.

Adele appears between louvered doors. It's
clearly Adele: that hair, the pointed nose, the silver chain that dips in the hollow of her throat.
What she's wearing starts just at her armpits and
hangs to the floor. A white terry-cloth thing. "I'll
take it from here, Mother," she says, which is a
whole lot more intimidating to me than to Mother.

I've never been fought over by two women,
and it doesn't exactly happen now. But they plant
me on a sofa so low I have to look out at the

world between my kneecaps, and Mother's in a velvet chair on one side, Adele on the other.

"Hi," I say to Adele, minutes too late. She rolls her green-gray eyes toward her mother, who's extended one brown leg in a gold sandal out through a slit in the orange terry cloth.

"I suppose you've seen the papers," Mrs. Parker says, replanting her hand. "The body in the bag? With the hand sticking out? Down by the bridge? Above Key Largo?"

"Mother," Adele says with immense emphasis, "they caught the killer."

"Well, I *know*." Mrs. Parker's hand climbs up to her throat. One red nail divides her chin. "I *read* it."

"Then you know Jim didn't do it. They don't get out on bail that soon."

"Oh, Adele, really." Her mother sighs and covers by turning her guns on me. We have a little give-and-take while she rechecks information: Van Cortlandt Academy, Brooklyn Heights, little brother, Summer with a Father. She tries to add to the slender store of knowledge, probes for a more recognizable family name than Atwater, learns Livingston, and nods. "And your father, he's in business down here?"

"Yes." This isn't enough. She waits. "In real estate."

She smiles, tosses her head, waves a hand. "Who isn't, down here? And your mother's in New York?"

I nod. In a manner of speaking she is, and I

have no intention of going into it. I've been going into things with people all day.

"Married again?"

I look at her, bone-tired.

"Is your mother married again?" she repeats, helping me.

"No, never again." I'm so tired I'll have to take my bike back in a cab.

"Oh, I know, I know." Both hands move in the air. "I can feel for her. The things you give up in a marriage and the little you get back." Her look flits over Adele, but she's treading on dangerous ground there and seems to know it. "Better a broken home than an unhappy one," she says, leaning confidentially my way. She's telling her daughter something for the thousandth time, this time through me.

"Hungry?" Adele says, skewering me with a look. This is a signal. It triggers Mother, who leaps out of her chair.

"Of course he is," she says. "I'll just see if I can find something." She glitters away through a dark dining room, propping a kitchen door open as she disappears through it.

"She's been arranging things on plates ever since you called," Adele murmurs.

"My mother's dead," I murmur back, which is a stupid and heavy thing to lay on her, sure to make her uncomfortable. She looks annoyed instead. I figure I have nothing to lose with these people. "So how's the summer going?" I say.

"Eight days till flight time," she says. "I will just make it." She states each word separately. "If

I don't get back to New York pretty soon, they're going to find another body in a bag down at Key Largo." This would be impressive except she's not looking at me as she speaks.

I try again. "What have you been doing with yourself?" This is a Spence mixer in isolation. There's no wall to get against.

"We drive to Bal Harbor and have lunch at Neiman's and then we shop," she says in a voice of the dead. "We drive downtown to Omni and have lunch at Jordan Marsh, and then we shop. We drive to Dadeland, and we have lunch at Burdine's, and then we shop." She rests a weary hand at her throat, over the silver chain. I've seen this gesture before.

"We'd better swim," she says, "or it'll be three in the pool."

"Do you want to go out somewhere?" I offer, but my heart isn't in it.

"That also would be a threesome," Adele says loud enough to be heard all over the house. She stands up and electrifies me briefly by unzipping an invisible zipper down her entire front. She's wearing a swimsuit underneath. "Just change anywhere," she says, starting to wave a hand at the louvered doors, but changes the wave to a pointing finger.

"Not in your room, darling!" her mother's voice sings out from the kitchen, ears on her like an Indian scout. "In the guest room!"

Adele closes her eyes. "Third door on your left."

By the time I come back, feeling naked in

trunks, the living room's empty, but the cocktail
table is covered with plates of meatballs, egg rolls,
cookie-cutter sandwiches, and more to come because Mother's back in the kitchen.

Adele's in the pool, lighted from beneath. Her
legs are wavery under water. She's wearing a bath-
ing cap, which is a turn-off. I hook my toes on
the side, and dive in, nothing show-off. She turns
on her back and drifts away. When I'm in the
deep end, she's in the shallow. We reverse. I miss
her in passing.

"Do you know Heidi Ames?" she says from a
distance.

"Who?" I look around in the pool, thinking
she's introducing someone.

"Heidi. Ames. Did I ask you before?"

"No." I say. "No."

"She's from Brooklyn Heights. Or some
heights."

Old Heidi isn't going to keep us afloat. I swim
down into the luminous water and break the surface in mid-pool. Adele, the water sprite, is way
down by the diving board, treading water. "An-
drea Barth?" she's asking as the water runs out of
my ears. "She's very close with the girl who lives
in the same building with that friend of yours."

"Kit Klein," I offer.

"Whoever. Do you know her?"

I stand up in the water, raise my hands to
heaven. "You're the only girl I know in the
world!" I announce. And with this show-stopper,
her mother materializes at poolside, giving me a
look. She's carrying a tray with two freezer-

chilled glasses on it: Fresca with lime wedges, it turns out.

She crouches gracefully and holds the tray out over the pool so we have to swim and walk toward her, to relieve her burden. "Drinks *in* the pool," she smiles, "like *Jamaica*." Gold chains swing out from her neck, dip over the water. "And something to nibble on inside when you're finished."

We're already finished; the whole evening's finished. But as Mother staggers up and disappears back through the glass wall—to stand behind the curtains?—I give it one more shot. You don't get instant rapport overnight, I reason. And think my thinking is getting fuzzy.

We're standing nipple-deep in the cool pool, holding frosted Fresca above the blue-Jell-O water. And I'm shriveled up inside my trunks. I haven't got the patience for a Spence girl tonight. It's like talking a jumper down off a ledge, and I haven't got the patience. But what's one more shot:

"You were great with my little brother. On the plane."

She's pulling a strap up and spilling part of her drink out of the other hand. "Oh, kids . . ." she says, not able to relate the concept to Spence/New York.

It takes twenty minutes to towel-dry without the sun. Still, the water runs down out of my trunks. Adele works a deal whereby she shimmies out of her suit inside her terry-cloth thing. And then just steps out of her suit, a black puddle on the tiles. I wrap my towel around my trunks, hoping it'll absorb the rest of the water.

We get through ten minutes by standing over the cocktail table, spearing meatballs with toothpicks and eating enough to make a respectable dent. I can feel water running between my toes. Then, looking into my old conversational grab bag and finding it empty, I go back to the guest room and get dressed.

It's a great house for lurking. I'm about to reappear through the louvered doors when I hear the tail end of some mother-daughter talk. ". . . just all right," Adele's saying through clenched teeth, "barely."

"Well, are you going to give him your number in New York?" her mother's asking. "I don't see why you shouldn't."

"Or why I should."

"If you leave this sort of thing to your father . . ."

"What sort of thing?"

"Your *social* life?"

"Is that what this is?" Adele sighs. "Oh, God."

I reappear, and they step apart.

There's a minor outburst of friendliness at the front door. Mother and daughter have joined up to see me off. Mother laughs at all the locks that have to be thrown, switched, jiggled, keyed to get the door open. She laughs all the way to the floor. I tell her thanks. "Good to see you," I tell Adele.

"See you," she says, or echoes, or something.

They walk me out to the last lock and form a

group in the gateway. Mother pushes her luck and wraps an arm temporarily around Adele's waist. They're a study in orange and white terry cloth, identical in the lawn light.

I have this feeling you have when you know you're never going to see people again, the need to observe a moment of truth. For an exit line I'd like to poke a finger at Adele and say, "You've got it all wrong here. *You're* the pain in the ass; your mother's only a minor irritation."

Instead, I'm walking backwards down the path, giving them a little salute with my flight bag. And they're giving me little waves back. Then the iron gate sighs shut. They could use a moat and a drawbridge.

And I find I can get back on my own power. I pump hard at the approaches to humpback bridges, drink in the greatest thing about Florida: that you can see clouds at night. Big thunderheads stand up over the palm trees, actually white in the night.

Then I know where I've been. I've been calling on Mrs. Got-Rocks, in the checkered flesh. And Miss Got-Rocks. But Marietta need never know. Why spoil her dream?

Fourteen

The door's open now, and we should be able to walk straight through it into the last days, without having to count them. What can stop us now?

I lie awake nights, fingers laced behind my head, going over events. Letting myself grieve a little, over Mom, over lost time. Balance this with plus factors. Put a few items on hold. I'd like to revise the entire Adele wipe-out into a joke. But it still stings, and the laugh track isn't there yet.

Even Grandmother turns up for review, stiff and remote as ever, almost. Twitching the see-through cane she refuses to lean on. But she's taken a quarter turn, and I see another side. We'll be back there with her soon, keeping the parlor free on Monday nights for the club to clear Nixon. I have these flashes of truth: it makes a lot of sense for Grandmother to center her cause on San Clemente. Dealing at a distance is safer, more clear-cut.

And Marietta. I'd like to talk her out of her restored cheeriness. I don't go up to the diner in these last mornings. This is understood. And at dinner, she never "lets on." If anything, she's friendlier, kinder to me than before. This hurts. But when we're talking about strong codes and the value of distance, she has a thing or two in common with Grandmother.

I even help Dad try to sell the last apartment, the eighty-nine-five number with the *Star Wars* decorating. We never actually sell the thing, but we encounter a lot of exotic browsers. And we work out a game plan. I point out the Features: nineteen-cubic-foot side-by-side freezer/refrigerator with icemaker, self-cleaning oven, splash panel above stainless-steel sink, mica cabinet top in powder room, etc. Brand-name products all. Dad talks easy financing, security system, pool privileges.

After an intense encounter with a non-English-speaking Peruvian woman and a husband, maybe hers, we collapse in our office. "We could go into business," I say, mopping my brow.

"We are in business," he says.

One-liners like that, to recognize the post-truce. We make no big deal over what we have going together. We save our extravagant claims for pushing the apartment.

I lie awake at night, in no hurry now, imagining I can hear Byron's silent lizards climbing his side of the wall. We'll have to give his room a thorough search before we leave. There's something nagging at me in the night. But I can't see it, put my finger on it. It's there, but I'm not ready for it. All the big moments seem behind us, where they ought to be.

I doze, half deaf now to the jungle sounds, the sudden rain that peppers the roof and blows into the bay. Then I'm awake again, and there's light under the door. It's like that first night of the summer. I think I hear the rise and fall of By-ron's breathing through the wall, but I get up to check on things anyway. Step stealthily into shorts, vaguely contemplate burglars, vaguely con-template how disappointed they'll be.

Dad's sitting out under the ceiling light, in pa-jama pants, hunched over the counter. He's got his hand around a coffee mug. His mind's elsewhere.

He doesn't see me there in the doorway. His hair's flattened in the back, standing up in front, a whitish thatch in the light. He's thick around the middle and in the upper arm. Brown shoulders fading to tan down the curve of his back. His head jerks my way, and his eyes don't know me at first.

"That stuff'll keep you up nights." I nod at the mug.

"That stuff has no effect one way or the other. Want some?"

I have the feeling I'm butting in, but I don't say no to him any more when yes is just as easy. I hang around the counter, swilling coffee. His face is clenched up, and his mind has slipped off some-where else again. So I'm free to study him.

Maybe he can't get a decent night's sleep on that

cockamamy pull-out sofa. And maybe this is the way to start. "That bed as uncomfortable as it looks?"

"Nothing wrong with that bed," he says. "I'll miss it—later."

He looks up and I recognize him finally. I see myself behind the lines around the eyes and the pockets underneath. The place he's missed shaving under his nose is the place I can never get to without nicking a nostril. Fairly routine features, but familiar. "Something wrong?" I say. I'm not about to go back to bed if he's got something he'll let me hear. We don't have that much time left, and the future's—still in the future.

He gives a little shrug, but it's more like a spasm. "I think they call it mid-life crisis." He tries to give the term a flip twist, but it falls flat.

"What?"

"Mid-life crisis. They write books about it now. Books, no cures."

"What . . . what's it like?"

He's rubbing his chin again with the back of his hand, a habit I haven't developed yet. He starts slow, talking mainly to himself. "You spend the first part of your life running after things— grades, girls, jobs, status, roles, whatever's going.

"Then you spend the next part playing out the hand that's been dealt you. They switch the rules, and you conform to that too. Then one day you catch yourself pulling back. You lose a job you think you deserve to keep. Or you get up one morning and you can't—knot your tie around another day like the one before. Or you can't go on living another five minutes with . . . people.

"You start running away. And, if you're like me, you keep running. The running becomes the main event.

"Then one day—in a room like this—you look over your shoulder to see if anything's gaining on you. And nothing's there."

I follow this, up to a point, fall behind. "Bad feeling?"

"Empty. When you let other people down, guess who you end up feeling sorry for?"

"Yourself?"

"You got it. How?"

"I don't know. When Mom died, the way she did, I thought maybe I'd let her down." This is coming to me in words for the first time. I let them roll. "I thought—back in my mind—maybe there was something I could have done or noticed. Maybe if I'd been home the night she—went out to the car . . ."

Dad looks up. "Don't do that to yourself. You shouldn't—"

"Neither should you," I say.

And still he's worried. There's something else, and we haven't come near it. It must be Marietta. I reach out for her and prop her up between us, for the last time. "You can start over," I tell him, "with Marietta."

He's shaking his head. He's been over that with himself, and he's a little impatient with me, like Byron gets. "I would if I could. She could breathe life back into a corpse. But that wouldn't work out."

"Why not?"

"Because Marietta's—in business for herself. She's come a long way from where she's been. There's something behind her Mrs. Got-Rocks daydreams. I don't mean she gives a damn for material things, but she wants to get someplace in life. If she marries anybody, it'll be a guy from a background she can understand. Some guy trading up. Going from blue collar to white. Going from driving a rig to owning a fleet. Somebody she can move up with. You must have noticed—she pities me."

I had and I hadn't. But I hate hearing him put it into words. I stand with my finger cramped into the mug handle and wonder if getting people to talk is such great therapy. But he's talking again, something about Byron.

"—hasn't he said anything to you?" Dad's squinting up at me through the light. "He wants to stay down here, with me."

No, I didn't hear that.

"I want you to know, I didn't influence him. He—"

Not much you didn't.

"—likes it down here. I could get him into a school. He's old enough to—"

He's a baby. He's confused a vacation with real life. Hell, yes, he likes it down here. He's gone native, wandering around in the jungle like Wolf Boy.

"—begin taking charge of himself. And I can

spend a lot of time with him. He's worried about what you'd think about it, Jim. He—"

He ought to be worried about what I'd think about it.

"—won't stay unless you say it's okay."

Then he won't stay.

"It's to late for you and me. But I could still be something for him, something more than just making up for lost time."

And still I haven't said anything. I've actually kept my mouth shut through all this, and the problem with that is: I've heard every word.

"I can't ask you to let me be his father, when I wouldn't be yours. But he needs one. And he'll still need one after you're away at college and grown up. I'll see him through. I promise you that."

At last I can say the word. "No." I slam the mug down, but I keep my voice under control. "No."

Fifteen

Senior year. Very crucial, and a drag. We're talking about the college application tension, and we're talking about Spence mixers populated by all the Adeles of this world, and their younger sisters: a whole new generation far from frost-free. And we're talking about Kit Klein lumbering out of his chrysalis as the Complete Ivy League Man: good-bye to buddydom; he's reading *Gentlemen's Quarterly* and looking for a pose. And he hasn't put in a summer like mine.

We're talking about the tall old brownstones of Brooklyn Heights, empty-eyed above their high stoops, and Grandmother's cane on the stairs on symphony night. And the West Side IRT express up to school every morning, with the same six girls in lengthening skirts who jiggle their buns out of the car at 72nd Street.

We're talking about the Lower School ball team

and Advanced Placement English and the Mickey
Mouse senior-slump courses. And the old school tie
which is splitting at the seams with the label hanging by a thread.

And we're talking about the year Byron stayed
down in Florida, the first year.

He was pretty watchful around me in those last
days. He took time out from his lizards to hang
out, waiting for a sign. I'd look over my shoulder,
and there he'd be, silent in sneakers. Brown, lanky,
"growing like a weed," in Marietta's well-worn
phrase. His legs are welted with mosquito bites;
his hair's bleaching out white at the ends. Scabs
on his elbows, Band-Aids on his knees, fingernails
like a dwarf coal miner's. I about had to wrestle
him to the ground to get him to put on socks and a
shirt so I could take him down to the store to get
him a size larger in everything. Though who
knows what they wear to school in Florida.

I don't even remember the moment when I
told him he could stay. It wasn't a touching scene.
I just said something like he was going to have to
start making a few decisions for himself, that I
was worn out making them for him. And all the
while his grin's getting bigger and bigger.

"Hell," I said, "I couldn't take you back to
New York looking like that anyway. You look
like a damn beach rat." He grunted approvingly at
himself and rubbed his chin with the back of his
hand.

"And when you learn to write, I want a letter
every week."

"I can write," he said. "I could write before I

even went to school!" Very indignant. Outraged, in fact.

"Then be sure you prove it. I need proof."

The day they take me to the airport, we swing by the diner. And Marietta, on cue, bursts out the door and across the sidewalk. She can make time in those blob shoes of hers. She is the breeze her apron tails snap in. She throws the car door open and jumps in to sit half on my lap. Locks her hands behind my neck. "You come back now, first chance you get." Her eyes are black violet. I've done the right thing is what she's really telling me. I'm not quite the snotty little smart-mouthed Yankee creep I seemed. I am redeemed within limits. "You'll get up Nawth," she says, earnest as anything, "and you'll get so hungry for grits it'll drive you half wild."

Then, sprightly to the end, she bobs forward to brush my cheek with her lips. But my arms are already around her, and I draw her in, shift my face, and I kiss her. A real kiss. "Whoooeee," she says when I let her move away, "what them New York girls have got in store!"

Then she's out of the car, bending down to look in the window. And I search her face for a sign of real sadness. She senses this, drops her head, sticks out her lower lip. A little parody of what she knows I'm looking for. Then a wink, and she's gone. Later, on the plane, I think of her. Working the counter for a road crew, queen of her little world and dreaming of a better one. And smiling difficult cases out the door.

The three of us, Dad, Byron, and I, hang
around the boarding lounge, waiting for the flight
to be called, the Nueva York Champagne flight.
Three men, as Marietta says, equals no conversation.

Byron's scratching a leg with the flat of his
other foot, and leaning against Dad for balance.
We should be laying last words on each other. Or
binding the break with plans for a Christmas re-
union. Byron's exploring around in his shorts
pocket. There may be wildlife in there somewhere. He's pretty anxious to get back to his
jungle.

They call the flight, and the boarding lounge
rises up in response. We shake hands, Dad and I,
Byron and I. But all around us the Latin Ameri-
cans are embracing, dropping their shopping bags
for a final kiss, a hug, a cry of good-bye. In a setting like this who's to notice if we put our arms
around each other? We have no history of hug-
ging, but who's to notice?

Dad puts his arms out. I put my arms out. We
grapple a little. Then step together for a moment,
Byron leaning against us both. We bang each
other on the back, make it hearty, make it quick.
Then we make the break.

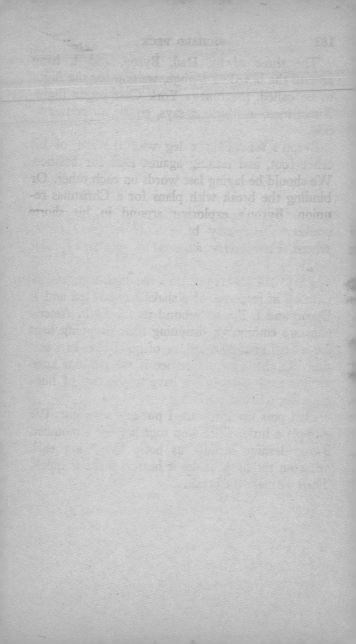